Roger Zelazny

The Hand of Oberon

AVON
PUBLISHERS OF BARD, CAMELOT, DISCUS AND FLARE BOOKS

AVON BOOKS
A division of
The Hearst Corporation
959 Eighth Avenue
New York, New York 10019

Copyright © 1976 by Roger Zelazny
Published by arrangement with Doubleday & Company, Inc.
Library of Congress Catalog Card Number: 75-39124
ISBN: 0-380-01664-8

First Avon Printing, June, 1977

AVON TRADEMARK REG. U.S. PAT. OFF. AND IN
OTHER COUNTRIES, MARCA REGISTRADA,
HECHO EN U.S.A.

Printed in the U.S.A.

WFH   10   9   8   7

A DAZZLING FUSION
OF MYTH AND
SCIENCE FANTASY
BY THE HUGO AWARD-WINNING
AUTHOR OF

NINE PRINCES IN AMBER
AND
SIGN OF THE UNICORN

Avon Books are available at special quantity discounts for
bulk purchases for sales promotions, premiums, fund raising
or educational use. Special books, or book excerpts, can also
be created to fit specific needs.

For details write or telephone the office of the Director of
Special Markets, Avon Books, 959 8th Avenue, New York,
New York 10019, 212-262-3361.

To Jay Haldeman,
of fellowship and artichokes.

The
Hand of
Oberon

1.

A bright flash of insight, to match that peculiar sun . . .

There it was. . . . Displayed within that light, a thing I had only seen self-illuminated in darkness up until then: the Pattern, the great Pattern of Amber cast upon an oval shelf beneath/above a strange sky-sea.

. . . And I knew, perhaps by that within me which bound us, that this had to be the real one. Which meant that the Pattern in Amber was but its first shadow. Which meant—

Which meant that Amber itself was not carried over into places beyond the realm of Amber, Rebma, and Tir-na Nog'th. Meaning, then, that this place to which we had come was, by the law of precedence and configuration, the real Amber.

I turned to a smiling Ganelon, his beard and wild hair molten in the merciless light.

"How did you know?" I asked him.

"You know I am a very good guesser, Corwin," he replied, "and I recall everything you ever told me about how things work in Amber: how its shadow and those of your struggles are cast across the worlds. I often wondered, in thinking of the black road, whether anything could have cast such a shadow into Amber itself. And I imagined that such a something would have to be extremely basic, powerful, and secret." He gestured at the scene before us. "Like that."

"Continue," I said.

His expression changed and he shrugged.

9

"So there had to be a layer of reality deeper than your Amber," he explained, "where the dirty work was done. Your patron beast led us to what seems to be such a place, and that blot on the Pattern looks to be the dirty work. You agreed."

I nodded.

"It was your perceptiveness rather than the conclusion itself which stunned me so," I said.

"You beat me to it," admitted Random, off to my right, "but the feeling has found its way into my intestines—to put it delicately. I do believe that somehow that is the basis of our world down there."

"An outsider can sometimes see things better than one who is part of them," Ganelon offered.

Random glanced at me and returned his attention to the spectacle.

"Do you think things will change any more," he asked, "if we go down for a closer look?"

"Only one way to find out," I said.

"Single file, then," Random agreed. "I'll lead."

"All right."

Random guided his mount to the right, the left, the right, in a long series of switchbacks which zigged us and zagged us across most of the face of the wall. Continuing in the order we had maintained all day, I followed him and Ganelon came last.

"Seems stable enough now," Random called back.

"So far," I said.

"Some sort of opening in the rocks below."

I leaned forward. There was a cave mouth back to the right, on level with the oval plain. Its situation was such that it had been hidden from sight when we had occupied our higher position.

"We pass fairly near it," I said.

"—quickly, cautiously, and silently," Random added, drawing his blade.

I unsheathed Grayswandir, and one turn back above me Ganelon drew his own weapon.

We did not pass the opening, but turned leftward once more before we came to it. We moved within ten or fifteen feet of it, however, and I detected an unpleasant odor which I could not identify. The horses must have done a better job of it, though, or been pessimists by nature, because they flattened their ears, widened their nostrils, and made alarmed noises while turning against the reins. They calmed, however, as soon as we had made the turn and begun moving away once again. They did not suffer a relapse until we reached the end of our descent and moved to approach the damaged Pattern. They refused to go near it.

Random dismounted. He advanced to the edge of the design, paused and stared. After a time, he spoke without looking back.

"It follows that the damage was deliberate," he said, "from everything else that we know."

"It seems to follow," I said.

"It is also obvious that we were brought here for a reason."

"I'd say so."

"Then it does not take too much imagination to conlude that our purpose for being here is to determine how the Pattern was damaged and what might be done to repair it."

"Possibly. What is your diagnosis?"

"Nothing yet."

He moved along the perimeter of the figure, off to the right where the smear-effect began. I resheathed my blade and prepared to dismount. Ganelon reached over and took hold of my shoulder.

"I can make it myself——" I began.

But, "Corwin," he said, ignoring my words, "there does appear to be a small irregularity out toward the middle of the Pattern. It does not look like something that belongs . . ."

"Where?"

He pointed and I followed the gesture.

There was some foreign object near the center. A stick? A stone? A stray bit of paper . . . ? It was impossible to tell from this distance.

"I see it," I said.

11

We dismounted and headed toward Random, who by then was crouched at the extreme right of the figure, examining the discoloration.

"Ganelon's spotted something out toward the center," I said.

Random nodded.

"I've noticed it," he replied. "I was just trying to decide on the best way to head out for a better look. I do not relish the notion of walking a broken Pattern. On the other hand, I was wondering what I would be laying myself open to if I tried heading in across the blackened area. What do you think?"

"Walking what there is of the Pattern would take some time," I said, "if the resistance is on par with what it is at home. Also, we have been taught that it is death to stray from it—and this setup would force me to leave it when I reach the blot. On the other hand, as you say, I might be alerting our enemies by treading on the black. So—"

"So neither of you is going to do it," Ganelon interrupted. "I am."

Then, without waiting for a reply, he took a running leap into the black sector, raced along it toward the center, paused long enough to pick up some small object, turned and headed back.

Moments later, he stood before us.

"That was a risky thing to do," Random said.

He nodded.

"But you two would still be debating it if I hadn't." He raised his hand and extended it. "Now, what do you make of this?"

He was holding a dagger. Impaled on it was a rectangle of stained pasteboard. I took them from him.

"Looks like a Trump," Random said.

"Yes."

I worked the card loose, smoothed down the torn sections. The man I regarded upon it was half familiar —meaning of course that he was also half strange.

12

Light, straight hair, a trifle sharp-featured, a small smile, somewhat slight of build.

I shook my head.

"I do not know him," I said.

"Let me see."

Random took the card from me, frowned at it.

"No," he said after a time. "I don't either. It almost seems as though I should, but . . . No."

At that moment, the horses renewed their complaints much more forcefully. And we needed but turn part way to learn the cause of their discomfort, in that it had chosen that moment to emerge from the cave.

"Damn," said Random.

I agreed with him.

Ganelon cleared his throat, took forth his blade.

"Anyone know what it is?" he asked quietly.

My first impression of the beast was that it was snakelike, both from its movements and because of the fact that its long thick tail seemed more a continuation of its long thin body than a mere appendage. It moved on four double-jointed legs, however, large-footed and wickedly clawed. Its narrow head was beaked, and it swung from side to side as it advanced, showing us one pale blue eye and then the other. Large wings were folded against its sides, purple and leathery. It possessed neither hair nor feathers, though there were scaled areas across its breast, shoulders, back, and along the length of its tail. From beak-bayonet to twisting tail-tip it seemed a little over three meters. There was a small tinkling sound as it moved, and I caught a flash of something bright at its throat.

"Closest thing I know," said Random, "is a heraldic beast—the griffin. Only this one is bald and purple."

"Definitely not our national bird," I added, drawing Grayswandir and swinging its point into line with the creature's head.

The beast darted a red, forked tongue. It raised its wings a few inches, then let them fall. When its head swung to the right its tail moved to the left, then left

13

and right, right and left—producing a near-hypnotic, flowing effect as it advanced.

It seemed more concerned with the horses than with us, however, for its course was directed well past us toward the spot where our mounts stood quivering and stamping. I moved to interpose myself.

At that point, it reared.

Its wings went up and out, spreading like a pair of slack sails suddenly caught by a gust of wind. It was back on its hind legs and towering above us, seeming to occupy at least four times the space it had previously. And then it shrieked, a god-awful, hunting scream or challenge that left my ears ringing. With that, it snapped those wings downward and sprang, becoming temporarily airborne.

The horses bolted and ran. The beast was beyond our reach. It was only then that I realized what the bright flash and the tinkling had represented. The thing was tethered, by means of a long chain running back into the cave. The exact length of its leash was immediately a question of more than academic interest.

I turned as it passed, hissing, flapping, and falling, beyond us. It had not possessed sufficient momentum to obtain true flight in that brief rush upward. I saw that Star and Firedrake were retreating toward the far end of the oval. Random's mount Iago, on the other hand, had bolted in the direction of the Pattern.

The beast touched ground again, turned as if to pursue Iago, appeared to study us once more, and froze. It was much nearer this time—under four meters —and it cocked its head, showing us its right eye, then opened its beak and made a soft cawing noise.

"What say we rush it now?" said Random.

"No. Wait. There is something peculiar about its behavior."

It had dropped its head while I was speaking, spreading its wings downward. It struck the ground three times with its beak and looked up again. Then it drew its wings part way back toward its body. Its tail twitched once, then swung more vigorously from side to side. It opened its beak and repeated the cawing sound.

At that moment we were distracted.

Iago had entered the Pattern, well to the side of the darkened area. Five or six meters into it, standing obliquely across the lines of power, he was caught near one of the Veil points like an insect on a piece of flypaper. He cried loudly as the sparks came up about him and his mane rose and stood erect.

Immediately, the sky began to darken directly overhead. But it was no cloud of water vapor which had begun to coalesce. Rather, it was a perfectly circular formation which had appeared, red at the center, yellow nearer the edges, turning in a clockwise direction. A sound like a single bell chime followed by the growl of a bull-roarer suddenly came to our ears.

Iago continued his struggles, first freeing his right front foot, then entangling it again as he freed the left, neighing wildly the while. The sparks were up to his shoulders by then, and he shook them like raindrops from his body and neck, his entire form taking on a soft, buttery glow.

The roaring increased in volume and small lightnings began to play at the heart of the red thing above us. A rattling noise caught my attention at that moment, and I glanced downward to discover that the purple griffin had slithered past and moved to interpose itself between us and the loud red phenomenon. It crouched like a gargoyle, facing away from us, watching the spectacle.

Just then, Iago freed both front feet and reared. There was something insubstantial about him by then, what with his brightness and the spark-shot indistinctness of his outline. He might have neighed at that moment, but all other sounds were submerged by the incessant roar from above.

A funnel descended from the noisy formation—bright, flashing, wailing now, and tremendously fast. It touched the rearing horse, and for a moment his outline expanded enormously, becoming increasingly tenuous in direct proportion to this effect. And then he was gone. For a brief interval, the funnel remained stationary, like a perfectly balanced top. Then the sound began to diminish.

The trunk raised itself, slowly, to a point but a small distance—perhaps the height of a man—above the Pattern. Then it snapped upward as quickly as it had descended.

The wailing ceased. The roaring began to subside. The miniature lightnings faded within the circle. The entire formation began to pale and slow. A moment later, it was but a bit of darkness; another moment and it was gone.

No trace of Iago remained anywhere that I could see.

"Don't ask me," I said when Random turned toward me. "I don't know either."

He nodded, then directed his attention toward our purple companion, who was just then rattling his chain.

"What about Charlie here?" he asked, fingering his blade.

"I had the distinct impression he was trying to protect us," I said, taking a step forward. "Cover me. I want to try something."

"You sure you can move fast enough?" he asked. "With that side . . ."

"Don't worry," I said, a trifle more heartily than necessary, and I kept moving.

He was correct about my left side, where the healing knife wound still ached dully and seemed to exercise a drag on my movements. But Grayswandir was still in my right hand and this was one of those occasions when my trust in my instincts was running high. I had relied on this feeling in the past with good results. There are times when such gambles just seem to be in order.

Random moved ahead and to the right. I turned sidewise and extended my left hand as you would in

16

introducing yourself to a strange dog, slowly. Our heraldic companion had risen from its crouch and was turning.

It faced us again and studied Ganelon, off to my left. Then it regarded my hand. It lowered its head and repeated the ground-striking movement, cawed very softly—a small, bubbling sound—raised its head and slowly extended it. It wagged its great tail, touched my fingers with its beak, then repeated the performance. Carefully, I placed my hand on its head. The wagging increased; its head remained motionless. I scratched it gently about the neck and it turned its head slowly then, as if enjoying it. I withdrew my hand and dropped back a pace.

"I think we're friends," I said softly. "Now you try it, Random."

"Are you kidding?"

"No, I'm sure you're safe. Try it."

"What will you do if you are wrong?"

"Apologize."

"Great."

He advanced and offered his hand. The beast remained friendly.

"All right," he said half a minute or so later, still stroking its neck, "what have we proved?"

"That he is a watchdog."

"What is he watching?"

"The Pattern, apparently."

"Offhand then," said Random, moving back, "I would say that his work leaves something to be desired." He gestured at the dark area. "Which is understandable, if he is this friendly to anyone who doesn't eat oats and whinny."

"My guess is that he is quite selective. It is also possible that he was set here after the damage was done, to defend against further unappreciated activity."

"Who set him?"

"I'd like to know myself. Someone on our side, apparently."

17

"You can now test your theory further by letting Ganelon approach him."

Ganelon did not move.

"It may be you have a family smell about you," he finally said, "and he only favors Amberites. So I will pass, thank you."

"All right. It is not that important. Your guesses have been good so far. How do you interpret events?"

"Of the two factions out for the throne," he said, "that composed of Brand, Fiona, and Bleys was, as you said, more aware of the nature of the forces that play about Amber. Brand did not supply you with particulars—unless you omitted some incidents he might have related—but my guess is that this damage to the Pattern represents the means by which their allies gained access to your realm. One or more of them did that damage, which provided the dark route. If the watchdog here responds to a family smell or some other identifying information you all possess, then he could actually have been here all along and not seen fit to move against the despoilers."

"Possibly," Random observed. "Any idea how it was accomplished?"

"Perhaps," he replied. "I will let you demonstrate it for me, if you are willing."

"What does it involve?"

"Come this way," he said, turning and heading over to the edge of the Pattern.

I followed him. Random did the same. The watchgriffin slunk at my side.

Ganelon turned and extended his hand.

"Corwin, may I trouble you for that dagger I fetched us?"

"Here," I said, drawing it from my belt and passing it over.

"I repeat, what does it involve?" Random inquired.

"The blood of Amber," Ganelon replied.

"I am not so sure I like this idea," Random said.

18

"All you have to do is prick your finger with it," he said, extending the blade, "and let a drop fall upon the Pattern."

"What will happen?"

"Let's try it and see."

Random looked at me.

"What do you say?" he asked.

"Go ahead. Let's find out. I'm intrigued."

He nodded.

"Okay."

He received the blade from Ganelon and nicked the tip of his left little finger. He squeezed the finger then, holding it above the Pattern. A tiny red bead appeared, grew larger, quivered, fell.

Immediately, a wisp of smoke rose from the spot where it struck, accompanied by a tiny crackling noise.

"I'll be damned!" said Random, apparently fascinated.

A tiny stain had come into being, gradually spreading to about the size of a half dollar.

"There you are," said Ganelon. "That is how it was done."

The stain was indeed a miniature counterpart of the massive blot further to our right. The watchgriffin gave forth a small shriek and drew back, rapidly turning his head from one of us to the other.

"Easy, fellow. Easy," I said, reaching out and calming him once more.

"But what could have caused such a large—" Random began, and then he nodded slowly.

"What indeed?" said Ganelon. "I see no mark to show where your horse was destroyed."

"The blood of Amber," Random said. "You are just full of insights today, aren't you?"

"Ask Corwin to tell you of Lorraine, the place where I dwelled for so long," he said, "the place where the dark circle grew. I am alert to the effects of those powers, though I knew them then only at a distance. These matters have become clearer to me with each

19

new thing I have learned from you. Yes, I have insights now that I know more of these workings. Ask Corwin of the mind of his general."

"Corwin," Random said, "give me the pierced Trump."

I withdrew it from my pocket and smoothed it. The stains seemed more ominous now. Another thing also struck me. I did not believe that it had been executed by Dworkin, sage, mage, artist, and one-time mentor to the children of Oberon. It had not occurred to me until that moment that anyone else might be capable of producing one. While the style of this one did seem somehow familiar, it was not his work. Where had I seen that deliberate line before, less spontaneous than the master's, as though every movement had been totally intellectualized before the pen touched the paper? And there was something else wrong with it—a quality of idealization of a different order from that of our own Trumps, almost as if the artist had been working with old memories, glimpses, or descriptions rather than a living subject.

"The Trump, Corwin. If you please," Random said.

There was that about the way in which he said it to make me hesitate. It gave rise to the feeling that he was somehow a jump ahead of me on something important, a feeling which I did not like at all.

"I've petted old ugly here for you, and I've just bled for the cause, Corwin. Now let's have it."

I handed it over, my uneasiness increasing as he held it in his hand and furrowed his brow. Why was I suddenly the stupid one? Does a night in Tir-na Nog'th slow cerebration? Why—

Random began to curse, a string of profanities unsurpassed by anything encountered in my long military career.

Then, "What is it?" I said. "I don't understand."

"The blood of Amber," he finally said. "Whoever did it walked the Pattern first, you see. Then they stood there at the center and contacted him via this

20

Trump. When he responded and a firm contact was achieved, they stabbed him. His blood flowed upon the Pattern, obliterating that part of it, as mine did here."

He was silent for the space of several deep breaths.

"It smacks of a ritual," I said.

"Damn rituals!" he said. "Damn all of them! One of them is going to die, Corwin. I am going to kill him—or her."

"I still do not—"

"I am a fool," he said, "for not seeing it right away. Look! Look closely!"

He thrust the pierced Trump at me. I stared. I still did not see.

"Now look at me!" he said. "See me!"

I did. Then I looked back at the card.

I realized what he meant.

"I was never anything to him but a whisper of life in the darkness. But they used my son for this," he said. "That has to be a picture of Martin."

2.

Standing there beside the broken Pattern, regarding a picture of the man who may or may not have been Random's son, who may or may not have died of a knife wound received from a point within the Pattern, I turned and took a giant step back within my mind for an instant replay of the events which had brought me to this point of peculiar revelation. I had learned so many new things recently that the occurrences of the past few years seemed almost to constitute a different story than they had while I was living them. Now this new possibility and a number of things it implied had just shifted the perspective again.

I had not even been aware of my name when I had awakened in Greenwood, that private hospital in upstate New York where I had spent two totally blank weeks subsequent to my accident. It was only recently that I had been told that the accident itself had been engineered by my brother Bleys, immediately following my escape from the Porter Sanitarium in Albany. I got this story from my brother Brand, who had railroaded me into Porter in the first place, by means of fake psychiatric evidence. At Porter, I had been subjected to electroshock therapy over the span of several days, results ambiguous but presumably involving the return of a few memories. Apparently, this was what had scared Bleys into making the attempt on my life at the time of my escape, shooting out a couple of my tires on a curve above a lake. This doubtless would have resulted in my death, had Brand not been a step behind Bleys and out to protect his insurance investment, me. He said he had gotten word to the cops, dragged me out of the lake, and administered first aid until help arrived. Shortly after that, he was captured by his former partners—Bleys and our sister Fiona—who confined him in a guarded tower in a distant place in Shadow.

There had been two cabals, plotting and counterplotting after the throne, treading on one another's heels, breathing down one another's necks, and doing anything else to one another that might suggest itself at that range. Our brother Eric, backed by brothers Julian and Caine, had been preparing to take the throne, long left vacant by the unexplained absence of our father, Oberon. Unexplained to Eric, Julian, and Caine, that is. To the other group, consisting of Bleys, Fiona, and—formerly—Brand, it was not unexplained because they were responsible for it. They had arranged for this state of affairs to come into being in order to open the way for Bleys's accession to the throne. But Brand had committed a tactical error in attempting to obtain Caine's assistance in their play for the throne, in that Caine decided a better deal obtained in upholding Eric's part. This left Brand under close scrutiny, but did not immediately result in the betrayal of his partners' identities. At about that time, Bleys and Fiona decided to employ their secret allies against Eric. Brand had demurred in this, fearing the strength of those forces, and as a result had been rejected by Bleys and Fiona. With everyone on his back then, he had sought to upset the balance of powers completely by journeying to the shadow Earth where Eric had left me to die centuries before. It was only later that Eric had learned that I had not died but was possessed of total amnesia, which was almost as good, had set sister Flora to watch over my exile, and hoped that that was the last of it. Brand later told me he had gotten me committed to Porter in a desperate move to

23

restore my memory as a preliminary to my return to Amber.

While Fiona and Bleys had been dealing with Brand, Eric had been in touch with Flora. She had arranged for my transfer to Greenwood from the clinic to which the police had taken me, with instructions to keep me narcotized, while Eric began arrangements for his coronation in Amber. Shortly thereafter, our brother Random's idyllic existence in Texorami was broken when Brand managed to send him a message outside the normal family channels—i.e., the Trumps—requesting deliverance. While Random, who was blissfully nonpartisan in the power struggle, was about this business, I managed to deliver myself from Greenwood, still relatively unmemoried. Having obtained Flora's address from Greenwood's frightened director, I betook myself to her place in Westchester, engaged in some elaborate bluffing, and moved in as a house guest. Random, in the meantime, had been less than successful in his attempt to rescue Brand. Slaying the snaky warden of the tower, he had had to flee its inner guards, utilizing one of the region's strangely mobile rocks. The guards, a hardy band of not quite human guys, had succeeded in pursuing him through Shadow, however, a feat normally impossible for most non-Amberites. Random had fled then to the shadow Earth where I was guiding Flora along the paths of misunderstanding while attempting to locate the proper route to enlightenment as to my own circumstances. Crossing the continent in response to my assurance that he would be under my protection, Random had come believing that his pursuers were my own creatures. When I helped him destroy them he was puzzled but unwilling to raise the issue while I seemed engaged in some private maneuver throneward. In fact, he had easily been tricked into conveying me back to Amber through Shadow.

This venture had proved beneficial in some respects while much less satisfactory in others. When I had finally revealed the true state of my personal situation,

Random and our sister Deirdre, whom we had encountered along the way, conducted me to Amber's mirror-city within the sea, Rebma. There I had walked the image of the Pattern and recovered the bulk of my memories as a result—thereby also settling the issue as to whether I was the real Corwin or merely one of his shadows. From Rebma I had traveled into Amber, utilizing the power of the Pattern to effect an instantaneous journey home. After fighting an inconclusive duel with Eric, I had fled via the Trumps into the keeping of my beloved brother and would-be assassin, Bleys.

I joined with Bleys in an attack on Amber, a mismanaged affair which we had lost. Bleys vanished during the final engagement, under circumstances which looked likely to prove fatal but, the more that I learned and thought about it, probably had not. This left me to become Eric's prisoner and an unwilling party to his coronation, after which he had had me blinded and locked away. A few years in the dungeons of Amber had seen a regeneration of my eyes, in direct proportion to the deterioration of my state of mind. It was only the accidental appearance of Dad's old adviser Dworkin, worse off mentally than myself, which had led to a way of escape.

After that, I set about recovering and I resolved to be more prudent the next time I went after Eric. I journeyed through Shadow toward an old land where I had once reigned—Avalon—with plans to obtain there a substance of which I alone among Amberites was aware, a chemical unique in its ability to undergo detonation in Amber. En route, I had passed through the land of Lorraine, there encountering my old exiled Avalonian general Ganelon, or someone very much like him. I remained because of a wounded knight, a girl, and a local menace peculiarly similar to a thing occurring in the vicinity of Amber herself—a growing black circle somehow related to the black road our enemies traveled, a thing for which I held myself partly responsible because of a curse I had pronounced at the time of my blinding. I won the battle, lost the girl, and traveled on to Avalon with Ganelon.

The Avalon we reached, we quickly learned, was under the protection of my brother Benedict, who had been having troubles of his own with a situation possibly akin to the black circle/black road menaces. Benedict had lost his right arm in the final engagement, but had been victorious in his battle with the hellmaids. He had warned me to keep my intentions toward Amber and Eric pure, and had then allowed us the hospitality of his manor while he remained for a few days more in the field. It was at his place that I met Dara.

Dara told me she was Benedict's great-granddaughter, whose existence had been kept secret from Amber. She drew me out as far as she could on Amber, the Pattern, the Trumps, and our ability to walk in Shadow. She was also an extremely skilled fencer. We indulged in a bit of casual lovemaking on my return from a hellride to a place where I obtained a sufficient quantity of rough diamonds to pay for the things I was going to need for my assault on Amber. The following day, Ganelon and I picked up our supply of the necessary chemicals and departed for the shadow Earth where I had spent my exile, there to obtain automatic weapons and ammunition manufactured to my specifications.

En route, we had some difficulties along the black road, which seemed to have extended its scope of influence among the worlds of Shadow. We were equal to the troubles it presented, but I almost perished in a duel with Benedict, who had pursued us through a wild hellride. Too angry for argument, he had fought me through a small wood—still a better man than I, even wielding his blade left-handed. I had only managed to best him by means of a trick involving a property of the black road of which he was unaware. I had been convinced that he wanted my blood because of the affair with Dara. But no. In the few words that passed between us he denied any knowledge of the existence of such a person. Instead, he had come after us convinced that I had murdered his servants. Now, Ganelon had indeed located some fresh corpses in the wood at Benedict's place, but we had agreed to forget about them, having no idea as to their identities and no desire to complicate our existence any further.

Leaving Benedict in the care of brother Gérard, whom I had summoned via his Trump from Amber, Ganelon and I proceeded to the shadow Earth, armed ourselves, recruited a strike force in Shadow, and headed off to attack Amber. But upon our arrival we discovered that Amber was already under attack by creatures which had come in along the black road. My new weapons quickly turned the tide in Amber's favor, and my brother Eric died in that battle, leaving me his problems, his ill will, and the Jewel of Judgment—a weather-controlling weapon he had used against me when Bleys and I had attacked Amber.

At that point, Dara showed up, swept on by us, rode into Amber, found her way to the Pattern, and proceeded to walk it—prima-facie evidence that we were indeed somehow related. During the course of this ordeal, however, she had exhibited what appeared to be peculiar physical transformations. Upon completion of the Pattern, she announced that Amber would be destroyed. Then she had vanished.

About a week later, brother Caine was murdered, under conditions arranged to show me as the culprit. The fact that I had slain his slayer was hardly satisfactory evidence of my innocence, in that the guy was necessarily in no condition to talk about it. Realizing, however, that I had seen his like before, in the persons of those creatures who had pursued Random into Flora's home, I finally found time to sit down with Random and hear the story of his unsuccessful attempt to rescue Brand from his tower.

Random, subsequent to my leaving him in Rebma years before, when I had journeyed to Amber to fight my duel with Eric, had been forced by Rebma's queen,

Moire, to marry a woman of her court: Vialle, a lovely blind girl. This was partly intended as a punishment for Random, who years before had left Moire's late daughter Morganthe pregnant with Martin, the apparent subject of the damaged Trump Random now held in his hands. Strangely, for Random, he appeared to have fallen in love with Vialle, and he now resided legendary unicorn of Amber.

After I left Random, I fetched the Jewel of Judgment and took it down to the chamber of the Pattern. There, I followed the partial instructions I had received for purposes of attuning it to my use. I underwent some unusual sensations during the process and was successful in obtaining control of its most obvious function: the ability to direct meteorological phenomena. After that, I questioned Flora concerning my exile. Her story seemed reasonable and jibed with those facts I did possess, although I had the feeling she was holding back somewhat on events at the time of my accident. She did promise to identify Caine's slayer as one of the same sort as those individuals Random and I had fought at her home in Westchester, however, and she assured me of her support in anything I might currently be about.

At the time I had heard Random's story, I was still unaware of the two factions and their machinations. I decided then that if Brand were still living, his rescue was of first importance, if for no other reason than the fact that he obviously possessed information that someone did not want circulated. I hit on a scheme for achieving this, the trial of which was only postponed for the time required by Gérard and myself for returning Caine's body to Amber. Part of this time, however, was appropriated by Gérard for purposes of beating me unconscious, just in case I had forgotten he was capable of the feat, to add weight to his words when he informed me that he would personally kill me should it turn out that I was the author of Amber's present woes. It was the most exclusive closed circuit fight I knew of, viewed by the family via Gérard's Trump—

an act of insurance should I actually be the culprit and have a mind to erase his name from the list of the living because of his threat. We journeyed on to the Grove of the Unicorn then and exhumed Caine. At that time, we actually caught a brief glimpse of the legendary unicorn of Amber.

That evening we met in the library of the palace in Amber—we being Random, Gérard, Benedict, Julian, Deirdre, Fiona, Flora, Llewella, and myself. There, we tested my idea for finding Brand. It amounted to all nine of us simultaneously attempting to reach him via his Trump. And we succeeded.

We contacted him and were successful in transporting him back to Amber. In the midst of the excitement, however, with all of us crowded about as Gérard bore him through, someone planted a dagger in Brand's side. Gérard immediately elected himself attending physician and cleared the room.

The rest of us moved to a downstairs sitting room, there to backbite and discuss events. During this time, Fiona advised me that the Jewel of Judgment might represent a hazard in situations of prolonged exposure, suggesting the possibilty that it, rather than his wounds, might have been the cause of Eric's death. One of the first signs, she believed, was a distortion of one's time-sense—an apparent slowdown of temporal sequence, actually representing a speed-up of physiological events. I resolved to be more cautious with it, in that she was more conversant with these matters than the rest of us, having once been an advanced pupil of Dworkin's.

And perhaps she was correct. Perhaps there was such an effect in operation later that evening when I returned to my own quarters. At least, it seemed as if the person who attempted to kill me was moving a trifle more slowly than I would have myself under similar circumstances. At that, the stroke was almost successful. The blade caught me in the side and the world went away.

Leaking life, I awoke in my old bed in my old home

on the shadow Earth where I had dwelled for so long as Carl Corey. How I had been returned, I had no idea. I crawled outside and into a blizzard. Clinging precariously to consciousness, I cached the Jewel of Judgment in my old compost heap, for the world did indeed seem to be slowing down about me. Then I made it to the road, to try flagging down a passing motorist.

It was a friend and former neighbor, Bill Roth, who found me there and drove me to the nearest clinic. There, I was treated by the same doctor who had attended me years before, at the time of my accident. He suspected I might be a psychiatric case, as the old record did reflect that faked state of affairs.

Bill showed up later, however, and set a number of things right. An attorney, he had grown curious at the time of my disappearance and done some investigating. He had learned about my fake certification and my successive escapes. He even possessed details on these matters and on the accident itself. He still felt there was something strange about me, but it did not really bother him that much.

Later, Random contacted me via my Trump and advised me that Brand had come around and was asking for me. With Random's assistance, I returned to Amber. I went to see Brand. It was then that I learned of the nature of the power struggle which had been going on about me, and the identities of the participants. His story, together with what Bill had told me back on the shadow Earth, finally brought some sense and coherence to occurrences of the past several years. He also told me more concerning the nature of the danger we currently faced.

I did nothing the following day, ostensibly for purposes of preparing myself for a visit to Tir-na Nog'th, actually to buy additional time in which to recover from my injury. This commitment made, however, it had to be kept. I did journey to the city in the sky that night, encountering a confusing collection of signs and portents, signifying perhaps nothing, and collecting a peculiar mechanical arm from the ghost of my brother Benedict while I was about it.

Returned from this excursion on high, I breakfasted with Random and Ganelon before setting out across Kolvir to return home. Slowly, bewilderingly, the trail began to change about us. It was as though we were walking in Shadow, a well-nigh impossible feat this near to Amber. When we reached this conclusion, we tried to alter our course, but neither Random nor I was able to affect the changing scene. About that time, the unicorn put in an appearance. It seemed to want us to follow it. We did.

It had led us through a kaleidoscopic series of changes, until finally we arrived at this pace, where it abandoned us to our present devices. Now, with this entire sequence of events tumbling through my head, my mind moved about the peripheries, pushed its way forward, returned to the words Random had just spoken. I felt that I was slightly ahead of him once more. For how long this state of affairs might last, I did not know, but I realized where I had seen work by the same hand which had executed the pierced Trump.

Brand had often painted when he was entering one of his melancholy periods, and his favorite techniques came to mind as I recalled canvas after canvas he had brightened or darkened. Add to this his campaign of years before to obtain recollections and descriptions from everyone who had known Martin. While Random had not recognized his style, I wondered how long it might be before he began thinking as I just had about the possible ends of Brand's information gathering. Even if his hand had not actually propelled the blade, Brand was party to the act by providing the means. I knew Random well enough to know that he meant what he had said. He would try to kill Brand as soon as he saw the connection. This was going to be more than awkward.

It had nothing to do with the fact that Brand had probably saved my life. I figured I had squared accounts with him by getting him out of that damned tower. No. It was neither indebtedness nor sentiment that caused me to cast about for ways to mislead Random or slow him down. It was the naked, frigid fact that I needed Brand. He had seen to that. My reason for saving him was no more altruistic than his had been in dragging me out of the lake. He possessed something I needed now: information. He had realized this immediately and he was rationing it—his life's union dues.

"I do see the resemblance," I said to Random, "and you may well be right about what happened."

"Of course I am right."

"It is the card that was pierced," I said.

"Obviously. I don't—"

"He was not brought through on the Trump, then. The person who did it therefore made contact, but was unable to persuade him to come across."

"So? The contact had progressed to a point of sufficient solidity and proximity that he was able to stab him anyway. He was probably even able to achieve a mental lock and hold him where he was while he bled. The kid probably hadn't had much experience with the Trumps."

"Maybe yes, maybe no," I said. "Llewella or Moire might be able to tell us how much he knew about the Trumps. But what I was getting at was the possibility that contact could have been broken before death. If he inherited your regenerative abilities he might have survived."

"Might have? I don't want guesses! I want answers!"

I commenced a balancing act within my mind. I believed I knew something that he did not, but then my source was not the best. Also, I wanted to keep quiet about the possibility because I had not had a chance to discuss it with Benedict. On the other hand, Martin was Random's son, and I did want to direct his attention away from Brand.

"Random, I may have something," I said.

"What?"

"Right after Brand was stabbed," I said, "when we were talking together in the sitting room, do you remember when the conversation turned to the subject of Martin?"

"Yes. Nothing new came up."

"I had something I might have added at that time, but I restrained myself because everyone was there. Also, because I wanted to pursue it in private with the party concerned."

"Who?"

"Benedict."

"Benedict? What has he to do with Martin?"

"I do not know. That is why I wanted to keep it quiet until I found out. And my source of information was a touchy one, at that."

"Go ahead."

"Dara. Benedict gets mad as hell whenever I mention her name, but so far a number of things she told me have proved correct—things like the journey of Julian and Gérard along the black road, their injury, their stay in Avalon. Benedict admitted these things had happened."

"What did she say about Martin?"

Indeed. How to phrase it without giving away the show on Brand . . . ? Dara had said that Brand had visited Benedict a number of times in Avalon, over a span of years. The time differential between Amber and Avalon is such that it seemed likely, now that I thought about it, that the visits fell into the period when Brand was so actively seeking information on Martin. I had wondered what kept drawing him back there, since he and Benedict had never been especially chummy.

"Only that Benedict had had a vistor named Martin, whom she thought was from Amber," I lied.

"When?"

"Some while back. I'm not sure."

"Why didn't you tell me this before?"

"It is not really very much—and besides, you had never seemed especially interested in Martin."

Random shifted his gaze to the griffin, crouched and gurgling on my right, then nodded.

"I am now," he said. "Things change. If he is still alive, I would like to get to know him. If he is not . . ."

"Okay," I said. "The best way to be about either one is to start figuring a way to get home. I believe we have seen what we were supposed to see and I would like to clear out."

"I was thinking about that," he said, "and it occurred to me that we could probably use this Pattern for that purpose. Just head out to the center and transfer back."

"Going in along the dark area?" I asked.

"Why not? Ganelon has already tried it and he's okay."

"A moment," said Ganelon. "I did not say that it was easy, and I am positive you could not get the horses to go that route."

"What do you mean?" I said.

"Do you remember that place where we crossed the black road—back when we were fleeing Avalon?"

"Of course."

"Well, the sensations I experienced in retrieving the card and the dagger were not unlike the upset that came over us at that time. It is one of the reasons I was running so fast. I would favor trying the Trumps again first, under the theory that this point is congruent with Amber."

I nodded.

"All right. We might as well try making it as easy as we can. Let's collect the horses first."

We did this, learning the length of the griffin's leash while we were about it. He was drawn up short about thirty meters from the cave mouth, and immediately set up a bleating complaint. This did not make the job of pacifying the horses any easier, but it did give rise to a peculiar notion which I decided to keep to myself.

Once we had things under control, Random located his Trumps and I brought out my own.

"Let's try for Benedict," he said.

34

"All right. Any time now."

I noticed immediately that the cards felt cold again, a good sign. I shuffled out Benedict's and began the preliminaries. Beside me, Random did the same.

Contact came almost at once.

"What is the occasion?" Benedict asked, his eyes moving over Random, Ganelon, and the horses, then meeting with my own.

"Will you bring us through?" I said.

"Horses, too?"

"The works."

"Come ahead."

He extended his hand and I touched it. We all moved toward him. Moments later, we stood with him in a high, rocky place, a chill wind ruffling our garments, the sun of Amber past midday in a sky full of clouds. Benedict wore a stiff leather jacket and buckskin leggings. His shirt was a faded yellow. An orange cloak concealed the stump of his right arm. He tightened his long jaw and peered down at me.

"Interesting spot you hie from," he said. "I glimpsed something of the background."

I nodded.

"Interesting view from this height, also," I said, noting the spyglass at his belt at the same time that I realized we stood on the wide ledge of rock from which Eric had commanded battle on the day of his death and my return. I moved to regard the dark swath through Garnath, far below and stretching off to the horizon.

"Yes," he said. "The black road appears to have stabilized its boundaries at most points. At a few others though, it is still widening. It is almost as if it is nearing a final conformity with some—pattern. . . . Now tell me, from what point have you journeyed?"

"I spent last night in Tir-na Nog'th," I said, "and this morning we went astray in crossing Kolvir."

"Not an easy thing to do," he said. "Getting lost on your own mountain. You keep heading east, you know.

That is the direction from which the sun has been known to take its course."

I felt my face flush.

"There was an accident," I said, looking away. "We lost a horse."

"What sort of accident?"

"A serious one—for the horse."

"Benedict," said Random, suddenly looking up from what I realized to be the pierced Trump, "what can you tell me concerning my son Martin?"

Benedict studied him for several moments before he spoke. Then, "Why the sudden interest?" he asked.

"Because I have reason to believe he may be dead," he said. "If that is the case, I want to avenge it. If it is not the case—well, the thought that it might be has caused me some upset. If he is still living, I would like to meet him and talk with him."

"What makes you think he might be dead?"

Random glanced at me. I nodded.

"Start with breakfast," I said.

"While he is doing that, I'll find us lunch," said Ganelon, rummaging in one of the bags.

"The unicorn showed us the way . . ." Random began.

3.

We sat in silence. Random had finished speaking and Benedict was staring skyward over Garnath. His face betrayed nothing. I had long ago learned to respect his silence.

At length, he nodded, once, sharply, and turned to regard Random.

"I have long suspected something of this order," he stated, "from things that Dad and Dworkin let fall over the years. I had the impression there was a primal Pattern which they had either located or created, situating our Amber but a shadow away to draw upon its forces. I never obtained any notion as to how one might travel to that place, however." He turned back toward Garnath, gesturing with his chin. "And that, you tell me, corresponds to what was done there?"

"It seems to," Random replied.

". . . Brought about by the shedding of Martin's blood?"

"I think so."

Benedict raised the Trump Random had passed him during his narration. At that time, Benedict had made no comment.

"Yes," he said now, "this is Martin. He came to me after he departed Rebma. He stayed with me a long while."

"Why did he go to you?" Random asked.

Benedict smiled faintly.

"He had to go somewhere, you know," he said. "He

37

was sick of his position in Rebma, ambivalent toward Amber, young, free, and just come into his power through the Pattern. He wanted to get away, see new things, travel in Shadow—as we all did. I had taken him to Avalon once when he was a small boy, to let him walk on dry land of a summer, to teach him to ride a horse, to have him see a crop harvested. When he was suddenly in a position to go anywhere he would in an instant, his choices were still restricted to the few places of which he had knowledge. True, he might have dreamed up a place in that instant and gone there—creating it, as it were. But he was also aware that he still had many things to learn, to ensure his safety in Shadow. So he elected to come to me, to ask me to teach him. And I did. He spent the better part of a year at my place. I taught him to fight, taught him of the ways of the Trumps and of Shadow, instructed him in those things an Amberite must know if he is to survive."

"Why did you do all these things?" Random asked.

"Someone had to. It was me that he came to, so it was mine to do," Benedict replied. "It was not as if I were not very fond of the boy, though," he added.

Random nodded.

"You say that he was with you for almost a year. What became of him after that?"

"That wanderlust you know as well as I. Once he had obtained some confidence in his abilities, he wanted to exercise them. In the course of instructing him, I had taken him on journeys in Shadow myself, had introduced him to people of my acquaintance at various places. But there came a time when he wanted to make his own way. One day then, he bade me good-by and fared forth."

"Have you seen him since?" Random asked.

"Yes. He returned periodically, staying with me for a time, to tell me of his adventures, his discoveries. It was always clear that it was just a visit. After a time, he would get restless and depart again."

"When was the last time you saw him?"

"Several years ago, Avalon time, under the usual circumstances. He showed up one morning, stayed for perhaps two weeks, told me of the things he had seen and done, talked of the many things he wanted to do. Later, he set off once more."

"And you never heard from him again?"

"On the contrary. There were messages left with mutual friends when he would pass their way. Occasionally, he would even contact me via my Trump—"

"He had a set of the Trumps?" I broke in.

"Yes, I made him a gift of one of my extra decks."

"Did you have a Trump for him?"

He shook his head.

"I was not even aware that such a Trump existed, until I saw this one," he said, raising the card, glancing at it, and passing it back to Random. "I haven't the art to prepare one. Random, have you tried reaching him with this Trump?"

"Yes, any number of times since we came across it. Just a few minutes ago, as a matter of fact. Nothing."

"Of course that proves nothing. If everything occurred as you guessed and he did survive it, he may have resolved to block any future attempts at contact. He does know how to do that."

"Did it occur as I guessed? Do you know more about it?"

"I have an idea," Benedict said. "You see, he did show up injured at a friend's place—off in Shadow—some years ago. It was a body wound, caused by the thrust of a blade. They said he came to them in very bad shape and did not go into details as to what had occurred. He remained for a few days—until he was able to get around again—and departed before he was really fully recovered. That was the last they heard of him. The last that I did, also."

"Weren't you curious?" Random asked. "Didn't you go looking for him?"

"Of course I was curious. I still am. But a man should have the right to lead his own life without the meddling of relatives, no matter how well-intentioned. He had pulled through the crisis and he did not attempt to contact me. He apparently knew what he wanted to do. He did leave a message for me with the Tecys, saying that when I learned of what had happened I was not to worry, that he knew what he was about."

"The Tecys?" I said.

"That's right. Friends of mine off in Shadow."

I refrained from saying the things that I might. I had thought them just another part of Dara's story, for she had so twisted the truth in other areas. She had mentioned the Tecys to me as if she knew them, as if she had stayed with them—all with Benedict's knowledge. The moment did not seem appropriate, however, to tell him of my previous night's vision in Tir-na Nog'th and the things it had indicated concerning his relationship to the girl. I had not yet had sufficient time to ponder the matter and all that it implied.

Random stood, paced, paused near the ledge, his back to us, fingers knotted behind him. After a moment, he turned and stalked back.

"How can we get in touch with the Tecys?" he asked Benedict.

"No way," said Benedict, "except to go and see them."

Random turned to me.

"Corwin, I need a horse. You say that Star's been through a number of hellrides . . ."

"He's had a busy morning."

"It wasn't that strenuous. It was mostly fright, and he seems okay now. May I borrow him?"

Before I could answer, he turned toward Benedict.

"You'll take me, won't you?" he said.

Benedict hesitated.

"I do not know what more there is to learn——" he began.

"Anything! Anything at all they might remember—possibly something that did not really seem important at the time but is now, knowing what we know."

Benedict looked to me. I nodded.

"He can ride Star, if you are willing to take him."

"All right," Benedict said, getting to his feet. "I'll fetch my mount."

He turned and headed off toward the place where the great striped beast was tethered.

"Thanks, Corwin," Random said.

"I'll let you do me a favor in return."

"What?"

"Let me borrow Martin's Trump."

"What for?"

"An idea just hit me. It is too complicated to get into if you want to get moving. No harm should come of it, though."

He chewed his lip.

"Okay. I want it back when you are done with it."

"Of course."

"Will it help find him?"

"Maybe."

He passed me the card.

"You heading back to the palace now?" he asked.

"Yes."

"Would you tell Vialle what has happened and where I have gone? She worries."

"Sure. I'll do that."

"I'll take good care of Star."

"I know that. Good luck."

"Thanks."

I rode Firedrake. Ganelon walked. He had insisted. We followed the route I had taken in pursuing Dara on the day of the battle. Along with recent developments, that is probably what made me think of her again. I dusted off my feelings and examined them carefully. I realized then that despite the games she had played

41

with me, the killings she had doubtless been privy or party to, and her stated designs upon the realm, I was still attracted to her by something more than curiosity. I was not really surprised to discover this. Things had looked pretty much the same the last time I had pulled a surprise inspection in the emotional barracks. I wondered then how much of truth there might have been to my final vision of the previous night, wherein her possible line of descent from Benedict had been stated. There was indeed a physical resemblance, and I was more than half-convinced. In the ghost city, of course, the shade of Benedict had conceded as much, raising his new, strange arm in her defense . . .

"What's funny?" Ganelon asked, from where he strode to my left.

"The arm," I said, "that came to me from Tir-na Nog'th—I had worried over some hidden import, some unforeseen force of destiny to the thing, coming as it had into our world from that place of mystery and dream. Yet it did not even last the day. Nothing remained when the Pattern destroyed Iago. The entire evening's visions come to nothing."

Ganelon cleared his throat.

"Well, it wasn't exactly the way you seem to think," he said.

"What do you mean?"

"That arm device was not in Iago's saddlebag. Random stowed it in your bag. That's where the food was, and after we had eaten he returned the utensils to where they had been in his own bag, but not the arm. There was no space."

"Oh," I said. "Then—"

Ganelon nodded.

"—So he has it with him now," he finished.

"The arm and Benedict both. Damn! I've small liking for that thing. It tried to kill me. No one has ever been attacked in Tir-na Nog'th before."

"But Benedict, Benedict's okay. He's on our side, even if you have some differences at the moment. Right?"

I did not answer him.

He reached up and took Firedrake's reins, drawing him to a halt. He stared up then, studying my face.

"Corwin, what happened up there, anyway? What did you learn?"

I hesitated. In truth, what had I learned in the city in the sky? No one was certain as to the mechanism behind the visions of Tir-na Nog'th. It could well be, as we have sometimes suspected, that the place simply served to objectify one's unspoken fears and desires, mixing them perhaps with unconscious guesswork. Sharing conclusions and reasonably based conjectures was one thing. Suspicions engendered by something unknown were likely better retained than given currency. Still, that arm was solid enough . . .

"I told you," I said, "that I had knocked that arm off the ghost of Benedict. Obviously, we were fighting."

"You see it then as an omen that you and Benedict will eventually be in conflict?"

"Perhaps."

"You were shown a reason for it, weren't you?"

"Okay," I said, finding a sigh without trying. "Yes. It was indicated that Dara was indeed related to Benedict—a thing which may well be correct. It is also quite possible, if it is true, that he is unaware of it. Therefore, we keep quiet about it until we can verify it or discount it. Understood?"

"Of course. But how could this thing be?"

"Just as she said."

"Great-granddaughter?"

I nodded.

"By whom?"

"The hellmaid we knew only by reputation—Lintra, the lady who cost him his arm."

"But that battle was only a recent thing."

"Time flows differently in different realms of Shadow, Ganelon. In the farther reaches— It would not be impossible."

He shook his head and relaxed his grip on the reins.

"Corwin, I really think Benedict should know about this," he said. "If it is true, you ought to give him a chance to prepare himself rather than let him discover it of a sudden. You people are such an infertile lot that paternity seems to hit you harder than it does others. Look at Random. For years, he had disowned his son, and now— I've a feeling he'd risk his life for him."

"So do I," I said. "Now forget the first part but carry the second one a step further in the case of Benedict."

"You think he would take Dara's side against Amber?"

"I would rather avoid presenting him with the choice by not letting him know that it exists—if it exists."

"I think you do him a disservice. He is hardly an emotional infant. Get hold of him on the Trump and tell him your suspicions. That way, at least, he can be thinking about it, rather than have him risk some sudden confrontation unprepared."

"He would not believe me. You have seen how he gets whenever I mention Dara."

"That in itself may say something. Possibly he suspects what might have happened and rejects it so vehemently because he would have it otherwise."

"Right now it would just widen a rift I am trying to heal."

"Your holding back on him now may serve to rupture it completely when he finds out."

"No. I believe I know my brother better than you do."

He released the reins.

"Very well," he said. "I hope you are right."

I did not answer, but started Firedrake to moving once more. There was an unspoken understanding between us that Ganelon could ask me anything he wanted, and it also went without saying that I would listen to any advice he had to offer me. This was partly because his position was unique. We were not related.

He was no Amberite. The struggles and problems of Amber were his only by choice. We had been friends and then enemies long ago, and finally, more recently, friends again and allies in a battle in his adopted land. That matter concluded, he had asked to come with me, to help me deal with my own affairs and those of Amber. As I saw it, he owed me nothing now, nor I him—if one keeps a scoreboard tally on such matters. Therefore, it was friendship alone that bound us, a stronger thing than bygone debts and points of honor: in other words, a thing which gave him the right to bug me on matters such as this, where I might have told even Random to go to hell once I had made up my mind. I realized I should not be irritated when everything that he said was tendered in good faith. Most likely it was an old military feeling, going back to our earliest relationship as well as being tied in with the present state of affairs: I do not like having my decisions and orders questioned. Probably, I decided, I was irritated even more by the fact that he had made some shrewd guesses of late, and some fairly sound suggestions based upon them—things I felt I ought to have caught myself. No one likes to admit to a resentment based on something like that. Still . . . was that all? A simple projection of dissatisfaction over a few instances of personal inadequacy? An old army reflex as to the sanctity of my decisions? Or was it something deeper that had been bothering me and was just now coming to the surface?

"Corwin," Ganelon said, "I've been doing some thinking . . ."

I sighed.

"Yes?"

". . . about Random's son. The way your crowd heals, I suppose it is possible that he might have survived and still be about."

"I would like to think so."

"Do not be too hasty."

"What do you mean?"

"I gather he had very little contact with Amber and

45

the rest of the family, growing up in Rebma the way that he did."

"That is the way I understand it, too."

"In fact, outside of Benedict—and Llewella, back in Rebma—the only other one he apparently had contact with would have been the one who stabbed him—Bleys, Brand, or Fiona. It has occurred to me that he probably has a pretty distorted view of the family."

"Distorted," I said, "but maybe not unwarranted, if I see what you are getting at."

"I think you do. It seems conceivable that he is not only afraid of the family, but may have it in for the lot of you."

"It is possible," I said.

"Do you think he could have thrown in with the enemy?"

I shook my head.

"Not if he knows they are the tools of the crowd that tried to kill him."

"But are they? I wonder . . . ? You say Brand got scared and tried to back out of whatever arrangement they had with the black road gang. If they are that strong, I wonder whether Fiona and Bleys might not have become *their* tools? If this were the case, I could see Martin angling for something which gave him power over them."

"Too elaborate a structure of guesses," I said.

"The enemy seems to know a lot about you."

"True, but they had a couple traitors to give them lessons."

"Could they have given them everything you say Dara knew?"

"That is a good point," I said, "but it is hard to say." Except for the business about the Tecys, which occurred to me immediately. I decided to keep that to myself for the moment though, to find out what he was leading up to, rather than going off on a tangent. So, "Martin was hardly in a position to tell them much about Amber," I said.

Ganelon was silent for a moment. Then, "Have you

had a chance to check on the business I asked you about that night at your tomb?" he said.

"What business?"

"Whether the Trumps could be bugged," he said. "Now that we know Martin had a deck . . ."

It was my turn to be silent while a small family of moments crossed my path, single file, from the left, sticking their tongues out at me.

"No," I said then. "I haven't had a chance."

We proceeded on for quite a distance before he said, "Corwin, the night you brought Brand back . . . ?"

"Yes?"

"You say you accounted for everyone later, in trying to figure out who it was that stabbed you, and that any of them would have been hard put to pull the stunt in the time involved."

"Oh," I said, "and oh."

He nodded.

"Now you have another relative to think about. He may lack the family finesse only because he is young and unpracticed."

Sitting there in my mind, I gestured back at the silent parade of moments that crossed between Amber and then.

4.

She asked who it was when I knocked and I told her.

"Just a moment."

I heard her footsteps and then the door swung in. Vialle is only a little over five feet tall and quite slim. Brunette, fine-featured, very soft-spoken. She was wearing red. Her sightless eyes looked through me, reminding me of darkness past, of pain.

"Random," I said, "asked me to tell you that he would be delayed a little longer, but that there was nothing to worry about."

"Please come in," she said, stepping aside and drawing the door the rest of the way open.

I did. I did not want to, but I did. I had not intended to take Random's request literally—that I tell her what had happened and where he had gone. I had meant simply to tell her what I had already said, nothing more. It was not until we had ridden our separate ways that I realized exactly what Random's request had amounted to: He had just asked me to go tell his wife, to whom I had never spoken more than half a dozen words, that he had taken off to go looking for his illegitimate son—the lad whose mother, Morganthe, had committed suicide, a thing for which Random had been punished by being forced to marry Vialle. The fact that the marriage had somehow worked beautifully was something which still amazed me. I had no desire to dispense a load of awkward tidings, and as I moved into the room I sought alternatives.

I passed a bust of Random set on a high shelf on the wall to my left. I had actually gone by before it registered that my brother was indeed the subject. Across the room, I saw her workbench. Turning back, I studied the bust.

"I did not realize that you sculpted," I said.

"Yes."

Casting my gaze about the apartment, I quickly located other examples of her work.

"Quite good," I said.

"Thank you. Won't you sit down?"

I lowered myself into a large, high-armed chair, which proved more comfortable than it had looked. She seated herself on a low divan to my right, curling her legs beneath her.

"May I get you something to eat, or to drink?"

"No thanks. I can only stay a short while. What it is, is that Random, Ganelon, and I had gotten a bit sidetracked on the way home, and after that delay we met with Benedict for a time. The upshot of it was that Random and Benedict had to make another small journey."

"How long will he be away?"

"Probably overnight. Maybe a bit longer. If it is going to be much longer he will probably call back on someone's Trump, and we'll let you know."

My side began to throb and I rested my hand upon it, massaging it gently.

"Random has told me many things about you," she said.

I chuckled.

"Are you certain you would not care for something to eat? It would be no trouble."

"Did he tell you that I am always hungry?"

She laughed.

"No. But if you have been as active as you say, I would guess that you did not take time for lunch."

"In that you would be only half-correct. All right. If

49

you've a spare piece of bread lying about it might do me some good to gnaw on it."

"Fine. Just a moment."

She rose and departed into the next room. I took the opportunity to scratch heartily all about my wound where it was suddenly itching fit to kill. I had accepted her hospitality partly for this reason and partly because of the realization that I actually was hungry. Only a little later it struck me that she could not have seen me attacking my side as I was. Her sure movements, her confident manner, had relaxed my awareness of her blindness. Good. It pleased me that she was able to carry it so well.

I heard her humming a tune: "The Ballad of the Water Crossers," the song of Amber's great merchant navy. Amber is not noted for manufacture, and agriculture has never been our forte. But our ships sail the shadows, plying between anywhere and anywhere, dealing in anything. Just about every male Amberite, noble or otherwise, spends some time in the fleet. Those of the blood laid down the trade routes long ago that other vessels might follow, the seas of a double dozen worlds in every captain's head. I had assisted in this in times gone by, and though my involvement had never been so deep as Gérard's or Caine's, I had been mightily moved by the forces of the deep and the spirit of the men who crossed it.

After a while, Vialle came in bearing a tray heavy with bread, meat, cheese, fruit, and a flask of wine. She set it upon a table near at hand.

"You mean to feed a regiment?" I asked.

"Best to be safe."

"Thanks. Won't you join me?"

"A piece of fruit, perhaps," she said.

Her fingers sought for a second, located an apple. She returned to the divan.

"Random tells me you wrote that song," she said.

"That was a very long time ago, Vialle."

"Have you composed any recently?"

50

I began to shake my head, caught myself, said, "No. That part of me is . . . resting."

"Pity. It is lovely."

"Random is the real musician in the family."

"Yes, he is very good. But performance and composition are two different things."

"True. One day when things have eased up . . . Tell me, are you happy here in Amber? Is everything to your liking? Is there anything that you need?"

She smiled.

"All that I need is Random. He is a good man."

I was strangely moved to hear her speak of him in this fashion.

"Then I am happy for you," I said. And, "Younger, smaller . . . he might have had it a bit rougher than the rest of us," I went on. "Nothing quite as useless as another prince when there is already a crowd of them about. I was as guilty as the rest. Bleys and I once stranded him for two days on an islet to the south of here . . ."

". . . And Gérard went and got him when he learned of it," she said. "Yes, he told me. It must bother you if you remember it after all this time."

"It must have made an impression on him, too."

"No, he forgave you long ago. He told it as a joke. Also, he drove a spike through the heel of your boot—pierced your foot when you put it on."

"Then it *was* Random! I'll be damned! I had always blamed Julian for that one."

"That one bothers Random."

"How long ago all of this was . . ." I said.

I shook my head and continued eating. Hunger seized me and she gave me several minutes of silence in which to get the upper hand on it. When I had, I felt compelled to say something.

"That is better. Much better," I began. "It was a peculiar and trying night that I spent in the sky-city."

"Did you receive omens of a useful nature?"

"I do not know how useful they might prove. On the

51

other hand, I suppose I'd rather have had them than not. Have there been any interesting happenings hereabouts?"

"A servant tells me your brother Brand continues to rally. He ate well this morning, which is encouranging."

"True," I said. "True. It would seem he is out of danger."

"Likely. It—it is a terrible series of happenings to which you have all been subjected. I am sorry. I was hoping you might obtain some indication of an upturn in your affairs during the night you spent in Tir-na Nog'th."

"It does not matter," I said. "I am not that sure of the value of the thing."

"Then why— Oh."

I studied her with renewed interest. Her face still betrayed nothing, but her right hand twitched, tapping and plucking at the material of the divan. Then, as with a sudden awareness of its eloquence, she stilled it. She was obviously a person who had answered her own question and wished now she had done it in silence.

"Yes," I said, "I was stalling. You are aware of my injury."

She nodded.

"I am not angry with Random for having told you," I said. "His judgment has always been acute and geared to defense. I see no reason not to rely on it myself. I must inquire as to how much he has told you, however, both for your own safety and my peace of mind. For there are things I suspect but have not yet spoken."

"I understand. It is difficult to assess a negative—the things he might have left out, I mean—but he tells me most things. I know your story and most of the others'. He keeps me aware of events, suspicions, conjectures."

"Thank you," I said, taking a sip of the wine. "It makes it easier for me to speak then, seeing how things are with you. I am going to tell you everything that happened from breakfast till now . . ."

So I did.

She smiled occasionally as I spoke, but she did not interrupt. When I had finished, she asked, "You thought that mention of Martin would upset me?"

"It seemed possible," I told her.

"No," she said. "You see, I knew Martin in Rebma, when he was but a small boy. I was there while he was growing up. I liked him then. Even if he were not Random's son he would still be dear to me. I can only be pleased with Random's concern and hope that it has come in time to benefit them both."

I shook my head.

"I do not meet people like you too often," I said. "I am glad that I finally have."

She laughed, then said, "You were without sight for a long while."

"Yes."

"It can embitter a person, or it can give him a greater joy in those things which he does have."

I did not have to think back over my feelings from those days of blindness to know that I was a person of the first sort, even discounting the circumstances under which I had suffered it. I am sorry, but that is the way that I am, and I am sorry.

"True," I said. "You are fortunate."

"It is really only a state of mind—a thing a Lord of Shadow can easily appreciate."

She rose.

"I have always wondered as to your appearance," she said. "Random has described you, but that is different. May I?"

"Of course."

She approached and placed her finger tips upon my face. Delicately, she traced my features.

"Yes," she said, "you are much as I had thought you would be. And I feel the tension in you. It has been there for a long while, has it not?"

"In some form or other, I suppose, ever since my return to Amber."

"I wonder," she said, "whether you might have been happier before you regained your memory."

"It is one of those impossible questions," I said. "I might also be dead if I had not. But putting that part aside for a moment, in those times there was still a thing that drove me, that troubled me every day. I was constantly looking for ways to discover who I really was, what I was."

"But were you happier, or less happy, than you are now?"

"Neither," I said. "Things balance out. It is, as you suggested, a state of mind. And even if it were not so, I could never go back to that other life, now that I know who I am, now that I have found Amber."

"Why not?"

"Why do you ask me these things?"

"I want to understand you," she said. "Ever since I first heard of you back in Rebma, even before Random told me stories, I wondered what it was that drove you. Now I've the opportunity—no right, of course, just the opportunity—I felt it worth speaking out of turn and order beyond my station simply to ask you."

A half-chuckle caught me.

"Fairly taken," I said. "I will see whether I can be honest. Hatred drove me at first—hatred for my brother Eric—and my desire for the throne. Had you asked me on my return which was the stronger, I would have said that it was the summons of the throne. Now, though . . . now I would have to admit that it was actually the other way around. I had not realized it until this moment, but it is true. But Eric is dead and there is nothing left of what I felt then. The throne remains, but now I find that my feelings toward it are mixed. There is a possibility that none of us has a right to it under present circumstances, and even if all family objections were removed I would not take it at this time. I would have to see stability restored to the realm and a number of questions answered first."

"Even if these things showed that you may not have the throne?"

54

"Even so."

"Then I begin to understand."

"What? What is there to understand?"

"Lord Corwin, my knowledge of the philosophical basis of these things is limited, but it is my understanding that you are able to find anything you wish within Shadow. This has troubled me for a long while, and I never fully understood Random's explanations. If you wished, could not each of you walk in Shadow and find yourself another Amber—like this one in all respects, save that you ruled there or enjoyed whatever other status you might desire?"

"Yes, we can locate such places," I said.

"Then why is this not done, to have an end of strife?"

"It is because a place could be found which *seemed* to be the same—but that would be all. We are a part of this Amber as surely as it is a part of us. Any shadow of Amber would have to be populated with shadows of ourselves to seem worth while. We could even except the shadow of our own person should we choose to move into a ready realm. However, the shadow folk would not be exactly like the other people here. A shadow is never precisely like that which casts it. These little differences add up. They are actually worse than major ones. It would amount to entering a nation of strangers. The best mundane comparison which occurs to me is an encounter with a person who strongly resembles another person you know. You keep expecting him to act like your acquaintance; worse yet, you have a tendency to act toward him as you would toward that other. You face him with a certain mask and his responses are not appropriate. It is an uncomfortable feeling. I never enjoy meeting people who remind me of other people. Personality is the one thing we cannot control in our manipulations of Shadow. In fact, it is the means by which we can tell one another from shadows of ourselves. This is why Flora could not decide about me for so long, back on the

55

shadow Earth: my new personality was sufficiently different."

"I begin to understand," she said. "It is not just Amber for you. It is the place plus everything else."

"The place plus everything else . . . *That* is Amber," I agreed.

"You say that your hate died with Eric and your desire for the throne has been tempered by the consideration of new things you have learned."

"That is so."

"Then I think I do understand what it is that moves you."

"The desire for stability moves me," I said, "and something of curiosity—and revenge on our enemies . . ."

"Duty," she said. "Of course."

I snorted.

"It would be comforting to put such a face on it," I said. "As it is, however, I will not be a hypocrite. I am hardly a dutiful son of Amber or of Oberon."

"Your voice makes it plain that you do not wish to be considered one."

I closed my eyes, closed them to join her in darkness, to recall for a brief while the world where other messages than light waves took precedence. I knew then that she had been right about my voice. Why had I trodden so heavily on the idea of duty as soon as it was suggested? I like credit for being good and clean and noble and high-minded when I have it coming, even sometimes when I do not—the same as the next person. What bothered me about the notion of duty to Amber? Nothing. What was it then?

Dad.

I no longer owed him anything, least of all duty. Ultimately, he was responsible for the present state of affairs. He had fathered a great brood of us without providing for a proper succession, he had been less than kind to all of our mothers and he then expected our devotion and support. He played favorites and, in fact, it even seemed he played us off against one another. He then got suckered into something he could not handle and left the kingdom in a mess. Sigmund Freud had long ago anesthetized me to any normal, generalized feelings of resentment which might operate within the family unit. I have no quarrel on those grounds. Facts are another matter. I did not dislike my father simply because he had given me no reason to like him; in truth, it seemed that he had labored in the other direction. Enough. I realized what it was that bothered me about the notion of duty: its object.

"You are right," I said, opening my eyes, regarding her, "and I am glad that you told me of it."

I rose.

"Give me your hand," I said.

She extended her right hand and I raised it to my lips.

"Thank you," I said. "It was a good lunch."

I turned and made my way to the door. When I looked back she had blushed and was smiling, her hand still partly raised, and I began to understand the change in Random.

"Good luck to you," she said, the moment my footsteps ceased.

". . . And you," I said, and went out quickly.

I had been planning to see Brand next, but just could not bring myself to do it. For one thing, I did not want to encounter him with my wits dulled by fatigue. For another, talking with Vialle was the first pleasant thing which had happened to me in some time, and just this once I was going to quit while I was ahead.

I mounted the stairs and walked the corridor to my room, thinking, of course, of the night of the knifings as I fitted my new key to my new lock. In my bedchamber, I drew the drapes against the afternoon's light, undressed, and got into bed. As on other occasions of rest after stress with more stress pending, sleep eluded me for a time. For a long while I tossed and twisted, reliving events of the past several days and some from even farther back. When finally I slept, my dreams were an amalgam of the same material, including a spell in my old cell, scraping away at the door.

It was dark when I awoke and I actually felt rested. The tension gone out of me, my reverie was much more peaceful. In fact, there was a tiny charge of pleasant excitement dancing through the back of my head. It was a tip-of-the-tongue imperative, a buried notion that—

Yes!

I sat up. I reached for my clothes, began to dress. I buckled on Grayswandir. I folded a blanket and tucked it under my arm. Of course . . .

My mind felt clear and my side had stopped throbbing. I had no idea how long I had slept, and it was hardly worth checking at this point. I had something far more important to look into, something which should have occurred to me a long while ago—had occurred, as a matter of fact. I had actually been staring right at it once, but the crush of time and events had ground it from my mind. Until now.

I locked my room behind me and headed for the stairs. Candles flickered, and the faded stag who had been dying for centuries on the tapestry to my right looked back on the faded dogs who had been pursuing him for approximately as long. Sometimes my sympathies are with the stag; usually though, I am all dog. Have to have the thing restored one of these days.

The stairs and down. No sounds from below. Late, then. Good. Another day and we're still alive. Maybe even a trifle wiser. Wise enough to realize there are many more things we still need to know. Hope, though. There's that. A thing I lacked when I squatted in that damned cell, hands pressed against my ruined eyes, howling. Vialle . . . I wish I could have spoken with you for a few moments in those days. But I learned what I learned in a nasty school, and even a milder curriculum would probably not have given me your grace. Still . . . hard to say. I have always felt I am more dog than stag, more hunter than victim. You might have taught me something that would have blunted the bitterness, tempered the hate. But would that have been for the best? The hate died with its object and the bitterness, too, has passed—but looking back, I wonder whether I would have made it without them to sustain me. I am not at all certain that I would have survived my internment without my ugly companions to drag me back to life and sanity time and again. Now I can afford the luxury of an occasional stagthought, but then it might have been fatal. I do not truly know, kind lady, and I doubt that I ever will.

Stillness on the second floor. A few noises from below. Sleep well, lady. Around, and down again. I wondered whether Random had uncovered anything of great moment. Probably not, or he or Benedict should have contacted me by now. Unless there was trouble. But no. It is ridiculous to shop for worries. The real thing makes itself felt in due course, and I'd more than enough to go around.

The ground floor.

"Will," I said, and, "Rolf."

"Lord Corwin."

The two guards had assumed professional stances on hearing my footsteps. Their faces told me that all was well, but I asked for the sake of form.

"Quiet, Lord. Quiet," replied the senior.

"Very good," I said, and I continued on, entering and crossing the marble dining hall.

It would work, I was sure of that, if time and moisture had not totally effaced it. And then . . .

I entered the long corridor, where the dusty walls pressed close on either side. Darkness, shadows, my footsteps . . .

I came to the door at the end, opened it, stepped out onto the platform. Then down once more, that spiraling way, a light here, a light there, into the caverns of Kolvir. Random had been right, I decided then. If you had gouged out everything, down to the level of that distant floor, there would be a close correspondence between what was left and the place of that primal Pattern we had visited this morning.

. . . On down. Twisting and winding through the gloom. The torch and lantern-lit guard station was theatrically stark within it. I reached the floor and headed that way.

"Good evening, Lord Corwin," said the lean, cadaverous figure who rested against a storage rack, smoking his pipe, grinning around it.

"Good evening, Roger. How are things in the nether world?"

"A rat, a bat, a spider. Nothing much else astir. Peaceful."

"You enjoy this duty?"

He nodded.

"I am writing a philosophical romance shot through with elements of horror and morbidity. I work on those parts down here."

"Fitting, fitting," I said. "I'll be needing a lantern."

He took one from the rack, brought it to flame from his candle.

"Will it have a happy ending?" I inquired.

He shrugged.

"I'll be happy."

"I mean, does good triumph and hero bed heroine? Or do you kill everybody off?"

"That's hardly fair," he said.

"Never mind. Maybe I'll read it one day."

"Maybe," he said.

I took the lantern and turned away, heading in a direction I had not taken in a long while. I discovered that I could still measure the echoes in my mind.

Before too long, I neared the wall, sighted the proper corridor, entered it. It was simply a matter of counting my paces then. My feet knew the way.

The door to my old cell stood partly ajar. I set down the lantern and used both hands to open it fully. It gave way grudgingly, moaning as it moved. Then I raised the lantern, held it high, and entered.

My flesh tingled and my stomach clenched itself within me. I began to shiver. I had to fight down a strong impulse to bolt and run. I had not anticipated such a reaction. I did not want to step away from that heavy brassbound door for fear that it would be slammed and bolted behind me. It was an instant close to pure terror that the small dirty cell had aroused in me. I forced myself to dwell on particulars—the hole which had been my latrine, the blackened spot where I had built my fire on that final day. I ran my left hand over the inner surface of the door, finding and tracing there the grooves I had worn while scraping away with my spoon. I remembered what the activity had done to my hands. I stooped to examine the gouging. Not nearly so deep as it had seemed at the time, not when compared to the total thickness of the door. I realized how much I had exaggerated the effects of that feeble effort toward freedom. I stepped past it and regarded the wall.

Faint. Dust and moisture had worked to undo it. But I could still discern the outlines of the lighthouse of Cabra, bordered by four slashes of my old spoon handle. The magic was still there, that force which had finally transported me to freedom. I felt it without calling upon it.

I turned and faced the other wall.

The sketch which I now regarded had fared less well than that of the lighthouse, but then it had been executed with extreme haste by the light of my last few matches. I could not even make out all of the details, though my memory furnished a few of those which were hidden: It was a view of a den or library, bookshelves lining the walls, a desk in the foreground, a globe beside the desk. I wondered whether I should risk wiping it clean.

I set my lantern on the floor, returned to the sketch on the other wall. With a corner of my blanket, I gently wiped some dust from a point near the base of the lighthouse. The line grew clearer. I wiped it again, exerting a little more pressure. Unfortunate. I destroyed an inch or so of outline.

I stepped back and tore a wide strip from the edge of the blanket. I folded what remained into a pad and seated myself on it. Slowly, carefully then, I set to work on the lighthouse. I had to get an exact feeling for the work before I tried cleaning the other one.

Half an hour later I stood up and stretched, bent and massaged life back into my legs. What remained of the lighthouse was clean. Unfortunately, I had destroyed about 20 per cent of the sketch before I developed a sense of the wall's texture and an appropriate stroke across it. I doubted that I was going to improve any further.

The lantern sputtered as I moved it. I unfolded the blanket, shook it out, tore off a fresh strip. Making up a new pad, I knelt before the other sketch and set to work.

A while later I had uncovered what remained of it. I had forgotten the skull on the desk until a careful stroke revealed it once again—and the angle of the far wall, and a tall candlestick. . . . I drew back. It would be risky to do any more rubbing. Probably unnecessary, also. It seemed about as entire as it had been.

The lantern was flickering once again. Cursing Roger for not checking the kerosene level, I stood and held the light at shoulder level off to my left. I put everything from my mind but the scene before me.

It gained something of perspective as I stared. A moment later and it was totally three-dimensional and had expanded to fill my entire field of vision. I stepped forward then and rested the lantern on the edge of the desk.

I cast my eyes about the place. There were bookshelves on all four walls. No windows. Two doors at the far end of the room, right and left, across from one another, one closed, the other partly ajar. There was a long, low table covered with books and papers beside the opened door. Bizarre curios occupied open spaces on the shelves and odd niches and recesses in the walls—bones, stones, pottery, inscribed tablets, lenses, wands, instruments of unknown function. The huge rug resembled an Ardebil. I took a step toward that end of the room and the lantern sputtered again. I turned and reached for it. At that moment, it failed.

I growled an obscenity and lowered my hand. Then I turned, slowly, to check for any possible light sources. Something resembling a branch of coral shone faintly on a shelf across the room and a pale line of illumination occurred at the base of the closed door. I abandoned the lantern and crossed the room.

I opened the door as quietly as I could. The room it let upon was deserted, a small, windowless living place faintly lit by the still smoldering embers in its single, recessed hearth. The room's walls were of stone and they arched above me. The fireplace was a possibly natural niche in the wall to my left. A large, armored door was set in the far wall, a big key partly turned in its lock.

I entered, taking a candle from a nearby table, and moved toward the fireplace to give it a light. As I knelt and sought a flame among the embers, I heard a soft footfall in the vicinity of the doorway.

Turning, I saw him just beyond the threshold. About five feet in height, hunchbacked. His hair and beard were even longer than I remembered. Dworkin wore a nightshirt which reached to his ankles. He carried an oil lamp, his dark eyes peering across its sooty chimney.

"Oberon," he said, "is it finally time?"

"What time is that?" I asked softly.

He chuckled.

"What other? Time to destroy the world, of course!"

5.

I kept the light away from my face, kept my voice low.

"Not quite," I said. "Not quite."

He sighed.

"You remain unconvinced."

He looked forward and cocked his head, peering down at me.

"Why must you spoil things?" he said.

"I've spoiled nothing."

He lowered the lamp. I turned my head again, but he finally got a good look at my face. He laughed.

"Funny. Funny, funny, funny," he said. "You come as the young Lord Corwin, thinking to sway me with family sentiment. Why did you not choose Brand or Bleys? It was Clarissa's lot served us best."

I shrugged and stood.

"Yes and no," I said, determined now to feed him ambiguities for so long as he'd accept them and respond. Something of value might emerge, and it seemed an easy way to keep him in a good humor. "And yourself?" I continued. "What face would you put on things?"

"Why, to win your good will I'll match you," he said, and then he began to laugh.

He threw his head back, and as his laughter rang about me a change came over him. His stature seemed to increase, and his face luffed like a sail cut too close to the wind. The hump on his back was diminished as he

64

straightened and stood taller. His features rearranged themselves and his beard darkened. By then it was obvious that he was somehow redistributing his body mass, for the nightshirt which had reached his ankles was now midway up his shins. He breathed deeply and his shoulders widened. His arms lengthened, his bulging abdomen narrowed, tapered. He reached shoulder height on me, then higher. He looked me in the eye. His garment reached only to his knees. His hump was totally resorbed. His face gave a final twist, his features steadied, were reset. His laughter fell to a chuckle, faded, closed with a smirk.

I regarded a slightly slimmer version of myself.

"Sufficient?" he inquired.

"Not half bad," I said. "Wait till I toss a couple logs on the fire."

"I will help you."

"That's all right."

I drew some wood from a rack to the right. Any stall served me somewhat, buying reactions for my study. As I was about the work, he crossed to a chair and seated himself. When I glanced at him I saw that he was not looking at me, but staring into the shadows. I drew out the fire-building, hoping that he would say something, anything. Eventually, he did.

"Whatever became of the grand design?" he asked.

I did not know whether he was speaking of the Pattern or of some master plan of Dad's to which he had been privy. So, "You tell me," I said.

He chuckled again.

"Why not? You changed your mind, that is what happened," he said.

"From what to what—as you see it?"

"Don't mock me. Even you have no right to mock me," he said. "Least of all, you."

I got to my feet.

"I was not mocking you," I said.

I crossed the room to another chair and carried it

over to a position near the fire, across from Dworkin. I seated myself.

"How did you recognize me?" I asked.

"My whereabouts are hardly common knowledge."

"That is true."

"Do many in Amber think me dead?"

"Yes, and others suppose you might be traveling off in Shadow."

"I see."

"How have you been—feeling?"

He gave me an evil grin.

"Do you mean am I still mad?"

"You put it more bluntly than I care to."

"There is a fading, there is an intensifying," he said. "It comes to me and it departs again. For the moment I am almost myself—almost, I say. The shock of your visit, perhaps . . . Something is broken in my mind. You know that. It cannot be otherwise, though. You know that, too."

"I suppose that I do," I said. "Why don't you tell me all about it, all over again? Just the business of talking might make you feel better, might give me something I've missed. Tell me a story."

Another laugh.

"Anything you like. Have you any preferences? My flight from Chaos to this small sudden island in the sea of night? My meditations upon the abyss? The revelation of the Pattern in a jewel hung round the neck of a unicorn? My transcription of the design by lightning, blood, and lyre while our fathers raged baffled, too late come to call me back while the poem of fire ran that first route in my brain, infecting me with the will to form? Too late! Too late . . . Possessed of the abominations born of the disease, beyond their aid, their power, I planned and built, captive of my new self. Is that the tale you'd hear again? Or rather I tell you of its cure?"

My mind spun at the implications he had just scattered by the fistful. I could not tell whether he spoke literally or metaphorically or was simply sharing paranoid delusions, but the things that I wanted to hear, had to hear, were things closer to the moment. So, regarding the shadowy image of myself from which that ancient voice emerged, "Tell me of its cure," I said.

He braced his finger tips together and spoke through them.

"I am the Pattern," he said, "in a very real sense. In passing through my mind to achieve the form it now holds, the foundation of Amber, it marked me as surely as I marked it. I realized one day that I am both the Pattern and myself, and it was forced to become Dworkin in the process of becoming itself. There were mutual modifications in the birthing of this place and this time, and therein lay our weakness as well as our strength. For it occurred to me that damage to the Pattern would be damage to myself, and damage to myself would be reflected within the Pattern. Yet I could not be truly harmed because the Pattern protects me, and who but I could harm the Pattern? A beautiful closed system, it seemed, its weakness totally shielded by its strength."

He fell silent. I listened to the fire. I do not know what he listened to.

Then, "I was wrong," he said. "Such a simple matter, too . . . My blood, with which I drew it, could deface it. But it took me ages to realize that the blood of my blood could also do this thing. You could use it, you could also change it—yea, unto the third generation."

It did not come to me as a surprise, learning that he was grandsire to us all. Somehow, it seemed that I had known all along, had known but never voiced it. Yet . . . if anything, this raised more questions than it answered. *Collect one generation of ancestry. Proceed to confusion.* I had less idea now than ever before as to what Dworkin really was. Add to this the fact which even he acknowledged: It was a tale told by a madman.

"But to repair it . . . ?" I said.

He smirked, my own face twisting before me.

"Have you lost your taste to be a lord of the living void, a king of chaos?" he asked.

"Mayhap," I replied.

"By the Unicorn, thy mother, I knew it would come to this! The Pattern is as strong in you as is the greater realm. What then is your desire?"

"To preserve the realm."

He shook his/my head.

" 'Twould be simpler to destroy everything and try a new start—as I have told you so often before."

"I'm stubborn. So tell me again," I said, attempting to simulate Dad's gruffness.

He shrugged.

"Destroy the Pattern and we destroy Amber—and all of the shadows in polar array about it. Give me leave to destroy myself in the midst of the Pattern and we will obliterate it. Give me leave by giving me your word that you will then take the Jewel which contains the essence of order and use it to create a new Pattern, bright and pure, untainted, drawing upon the stuff of your own being while the legions of chaos attempt to distract you on every side. Promise me that and let me end it, for broken as I am, I would rather die for order than live for it. What say you now?"

"Would it not be better to try mending the one we've got than to undo the work of eons?"

"Coward!" he cried, leaping to his feet. "I knew you would say that again!"

"Well, wouldn't it?"

He began to pace.

"How many times have we been through this?" he asked. "Nothing has changed! You are afraid to try it!"

"Perhaps," I said. "But do you not feel that something for which you have given so much is worth some effort—some additional sacrifice—if there is even a possibility of saving it?"

"You still do not understand," he said. "I cannot but

think that a damaged thing should be destroyed—and hopefully replaced. The nature of my personal injury is such that I cannot envision repair. I am damaged in just this fashion. My feelings are foreordained."

"If the Jewel can create a new Pattern, why will it not serve to repair the old one, end our troubles, heal your spirit?"

He approached and stood before me.

"Where is your memory?" he said. "You know that it would be infinitely more difficult to repair the damage than it would be to start over again. Even the Jewel could more easily destroy it than repair it. Have your forgotten what it is like out there?" He gestured toward the wall behind him. "Do you want to go and look at it again?"

"Yes," I said. "I would like that. Let's go."

I rose and looked down at him. His control over his form had begun slipping when he had grown angry. He had already lost three or four inches in height, the image of my face was melting back into his gnome-like features, and a noticeable bulge was growing between his shoulders, had already been visible when he had gestured.

His eyes widened and he studied my face.

"You really mean it," he said after a moment. "All right, then. Let us go."

He turned and moved toward the big metal door. I followed him. He used both hands to turn the key. Then he threw his weight against it. I moved to help him, but he brushed me aside with extraordinary strength before giving the door a final shove. It made a grating noise and moved outward into a fully opened position. I was immediately struck by a strange, somehow familiar odor.

Dworkin stepped through and paused. He located what looked to be a long staff leaning against the wall off to his right. He struck it several times against the ground and its upper end began to glow. It lit up the area fairly well, revealing a narrow tunnel into which he now advanced. I followed him and it widened before too long, so that I was able to come abreast of him. The odor grew stronger, and I could almost place it. It had been something fairly recent . . .

It was close to eighty paces before our way took a turn to the left and upward. We passed then through a little appendixlike area. It was strewn with broken bones, and a large metal ring was set in the rock a couple of feet above the floor. Affixed thereto was a glittering chain, which fell to the floor and trailed on ahead like a line of molten droplets cooling in the gloom.

Our way narrowed again after that and Dworkin took the lead once more. After a brief time, he turned an abrupt corner and I heard him muttering. I nearly ran into him when I made the turn myself. He was crouched down and groping with his left hand inside a shadowy cleft. When I heard the soft cawing noise and saw that the chain vanished into the opening I realized what it was and where we were.

"Good Wixer," I heard him say. "I am not going far. It is all right, good Wixer. Here is something to chew on."

From where he had fetched whatever he tossed the beast, I do not know. But the purple griffin, which I had now advanced far enough to glimpse as it stirred within its lair, accepted the offering with a toss of its head and a series of crunching noises.

Dworkin grinned up at me.

"Surprised?" he asked.

"At what?"

"You thought I was afraid of him. You thought I would never make friends with him. You set him out here to keep me in there—away from the Pattern."

"Did I ever say that?"

"You did not have to. I am not a fool."

"Have it your way," I said.

He chuckled, rose, and continued on along the passageway.

I followed and it grew level underfoot once again. The ceiling rose and the way widened. At length, we came to the cave mouth. Dworkin stood for a moment silhouetted, staff raised before him. It was night outside, and a clean salt smell swept the musk from my nostrils.

Another moment, and he moved forward once more, passing into a world of sky-candles and blue velours. Continuing after him, I had gasped briefly at that amazing view. It was not simply that the stars in the moonless, cloudless sky blazed with a preternatural brilliance, nor that the distinction between sky and sea had once again been totally obliterated. It was that the Pattern glowed an almost acetylene blue by that sky-sea, and all of the stars above, beside, and below were arrayed with a geometric precision, forming a fantastic, oblique latticework which, more than anything else, gave the impression that we hung in the midst of a cosmic web where the Pattern was the true center, the rest of the radiant meshwork a precise consequence of its existence, configuration, position.

Dworkin continued on down to the Pattern, right up to the edge beside the darkened area. He waved his staff over it and turned to look at me just as I came near.

"There you are," he announced, "the hole in my mind. I can no longer think through it, only around it. I no longer know what must be done to repair something I now lack. If you think that you can do it, you must be willing to lay yourself open to instant destruction each time you depart the Pattern to cross the break. Not destruction by the dark portion. Destruction by the Pattern itself when you break the circuit. The Jewel may or may not sustain you. I do not know. But it will not grow easier. It will become more difficult with each circuit, and your strength will be lessening all the while. The last time we discussed it you were afraid. Do you mean to say you have grown bolder since then?"

"Perhaps," I said. "You see no other way?"

"I know it can be done starting with a clean slate, because once I did it so. Beyond that, I see no other

71

way. The longer you wait the more the situation worsens. Why not fetch the Jewel and lend me your blade, son? I see no better way."

"No," I said. "I must know more. Tell me again how the damage was done."

"I still do not know which of your children shed our blood on this spot, if this is what you mean. It was done. Let it go at that. Our darker natures came forth strongly in them. It must be that they are too close to the chaos from which we sprang, growing without the exercises of will we endured in defeating it. I had thought that the ritual of traveling the Pattern might suffice for them. I could think of nothing stronger. Yet it failed. They strike out against everything. They seek to destroy the Pattern itself."

"If we succeed in making a fresh start, might not these events simply repeat themselves?"

"I do not know. But what choice have we other than failure and a return to chaos?"

"What will become of them if we try for a new beginning?"

He was silent for a long while. Then he shrugged.

"I cannot tell."

"What would another generation have been like?"

He chuckled.

"How can such a question be answered? I have no idea."

I withdrew the mutilated Trump and passed it to him. He regarded it near the blaze of his staff.

"I believe it is Random's son Martin," I said, "he whose blood was spilled here. I have no idea whether he still lives. What do you think he might have amounted to?"

He looked back out over the Pattern.

"So this is the object which decorated it," he said. "How did you fetch it forth?"

"It was gotten," I said. "It is not your work, is it?"

"Of course not. I have never set eyes on the boy. But this answers your question, does it not? If there is another generation, your children will destroy it."

72

"As we would destroy them?"

He met my eyes and peered.

"Is it that you are suddenly becoming a doting father?" he asked.

"If you did not prepare that Trump, who did?"

He glanced down and flicked it with his fingernail.

"My best pupil. Your son Brand. That is his style. See what they do as soon as they gain a little power? Would any of them offer their lives to preserve the realm, to restore the Pattern?"

"Probably," I said. "Probably Benedict, Gérard, Random, Corwin . . ."

"Benedict has the mark of doom upon him, Gérard possesses the will but not the wit, Random lacks courage and determination. Corwin . . . Is he not out of favor and out of sight?"

My thoughts returned to our last meeting, when he had helped me to escape from my cell to Cabra. It occurred to me that he might have had second thoughts concerning that, not having been aware of the circumstances which had put me there.

"Is that why you have taken his form?" he went on. "Is this some manner of rebuke? Are you testing me again?"

"He is neither out of favor nor sight," I said, "though he has enemies among the family and elsewhere. He would attempt anything to preserve the realm. How do you see his chances?"

"Has he not been away for a long while?"

"Yes."

"Then he might have changed. I do not know."

"I believe he is changed. I know that he is willing to try."

He stared at me again, and he kept staring.

"You are not Oberon," he said at length.

"No."

"You are he whom I see before me."

"No more, no less."

"I see. . . . I did not realize that you knew of this place."

"I didn't, until recently. The first time that I came here I was led by the unicorn."

His eyes widened.

"That is—very—interesting," he said. "It has been so long . . ."

"What of my question?"

"Eh? Question? What question?"

"My chances. Do you think I might be able to repair the Pattern?"

He advanced slowly, and reaching up, placed his right hand on my shoulder. The staff tilted in his other hand as he did so; its blue light flared within a foot of my face, but I felt no heat. He looked into my eyes.

"You have changed," he said, after a time.

"Enough," I asked, "to do the job?"

He looked away.

"Perhaps enough to make it worth trying," he said, "even if we are foredoomed to failure."

"Will you help me?"

"I do not know," he said, "that I will be able. This thing with my moods, my thoughts—it comes and it goes. Even now, I feel some of my control slipping away. The excitement, perhaps. . . . We had best get back inside."

I heard a clinking noise at my back. When I turned, the griffin was there, his head swinging slowly from left to right, his tail from right to left, his tongue darting. He began to circle us, halting when he came to a position between Dworkin and the Pattern.

"He knows," Dworkin said. "He can sense it when I begin to change. He will not let me near the Pattern then. . . . Good Wixer. We are returning now. It is all right. . . . Come, Corwin."

We headed back toward the cave mouth and Wixer followed, a clink for every pace.

"The Jewel," I said, "the Jewel of Judgment . . . you say that it is necessary for the repair of the Pattern?"

"Yes," he said. "It would have to be borne the entire distance through the Pattern, reinscribing the original design in the places where it has been broken. This

74

could only be done by one who is attuned to the Jewel, though."

"I am attuned to the Jewel," I said.

"How?" he asked, halting.

Wixer made a cackling noise behind us, and we resumed walking.

"I followed your written instructions—and Eric's verbal ones," I said. "I took it with me to the center of the Pattern and projected myself through it."

"I see," he said. "How did you obtain it?"

"From Eric, on his deathbed."

We entered the cave.

"You have it now?"

"I was forced to cache it in a place off in Shadow."

"I would suggest you retrieve it quickly and bring it here or take it back to the palace. It is best kept near the center of things."

"Why is that?"

"It tends to have a distorting effect on shadows if it lies too long among them."

"Distorting? In what fashion?"

"There is no way to tell, in advance. It depends entirely upon the locale."

We rounded a corner, continued on back through the gloom.

"What does it mean," I said, "when you are wearing the Jewel and everything begins to slow down about you? Fiona warned me that this was dangerous, but she was not certain why."

"It means that you have reached the bounds of your own existence, that your energies will shortly be exhausted, that you will die unless you do something quickly."

"What is that?"

"Begin to draw power from the Pattern itself—the primal Pattern within the Jewel."

"How is this achieved?"

"You must surrender to it, release yourself, blot out

75

your identity, erase the bounds which separate you from everything else."

"It sounds easier said than done."

"But it can be done, and it is the only way."

I shook my head. We moved on, coming at last to the big door. Dworkin extinguished the staff and leaned it against the wall. We entered and he secured the door. Wixer had stationed himself just outside.

"You will have to leave now," Dworkin said.

"But there are many more things that I must ask you, and some that I would like to tell you."

"My thoughts grow meaningless, and your words would be wasted. Tomorrow night, or the next, or the next. Hurry! Go!"

"Why the rush?"

"I may harm you when the change comes over me. I am holding it back by main will now. Depart!"

"I do not know how. I know how to get here, but—"

"There are all manner of special Trumps in the desk in the next room. Take the light! Go anywhere! Get out of here!"

I was about to protest that I hardly feared any physical violence he could muster, when his features began to flow like melting wax and he somehow seemed much larger and longer-limbed than he had been. Seizing the light, I fled the room, a sudden chill upon me.

. . . To the desk. I tore open the drawer and snatched at some Trumps which lay scattered within it. I heard footsteps then, of something entering the room behind me, coming from the chamber I had just departed. They did not seem like the footsteps of a man. I did not look back. Instead, I raised the cards before me and regarded the one on top. It was an unfamiliar scene, but I opened my mind immediately and reached for it. A mountain crag, something indistinct beyond it, a strangely stippled sky, a scattering of stars to the left . . . The card was alternately hot and cold to my touch, and a heavy wind seemed to come blowing through it as I stared, somehow rearranging the prospect.

From right behind me then, the heavily altered but still recognizable voice of Dworkin spoke: "Fool! You have chosen the land of your doom!"

A great clawlike hand—black, leathery, gnarled—reached over my shoulder, as if to snatch the card away. But the vision seemed ready, and I rushed forward into it, turning the card from me as soon as I realized I had made my escape. Then I halted and stood stockstill, to let my senses adjust to the new locale.

I knew. From snatches of legend, bits of family gossip, and from a general feeling which came over me, I knew the place to which I had come. It was with full certainty as to identity that I raised my eyes to look upon the Courts of Chaos.

6.

Where? The senses are such uncertain things, and now
mine were strained beyond their limits. The rock on
which I stood . . . If I attempted to fix my gaze upon it,
it took on the aspect of a pavement on a hot afternoon.
It seemed to shift and waver, though my footing was
undisturbed. And it was undecided as to the portion
of the spectrum it might call home. It pulsated and
flashed like the skin of an iguana. Looking upward, I
beheld a sky such as I had never before set eyes upon.
At the moment, it was split down the middle—half of
it of deepest night-black, and the stars danced within
it. When I say danced, I do not mean twinkled; they
cavorted and they shifted magnitudes; they darted and
they circled; they flared to nova brilliance, then faded
to nothing. It was a frightening spectacle to behold, and
my stomach tightened within me as I experienced a
profound acrophobia. Yet, shifting my gaze did little to
improve the situation. The other half of the sky was
like a bottle of colored sands, continuously shaken;
belts of orange, yellow, red, blue, brown, and purple
turned and twisted; patches of green, mauve, gray, and
dead white came and went, sometimes snaking into
belthood, replacing or joining the other writhing enti-
ties. And these, too, shimmered and wavered, creating
impossible sensations of distance and nearness. At
times, some or all seemed literally sky-high, and then
again they came to fill the air before me, gauzy,
transparent mists, translucent swaths or solid tentacles

78

of color. It was not until later that I realized that the line which separated the black from the color was advancing slowly from my right while retreating to my left. It was as if the entire celestial mandala were rotating about a point directly overhead. As to the light source of the brighter half, it simply could not be determined. Standing there, I looked down upon what at first seemed a valley filled with countless explosions of color; but when the advancing darkness faced this display away the stars danced and burned within its depths as well as above, giving them the impression of a bottomless chasm. It was as if I stood at the end of the world, the end of the universe, the end of everything. But far, far out from where I stood, something hovered on a mount of sheerest black—a blackness itself, but edged and tempered with barely perceptible flashes of light. I could not guess at its size, for distance, depth, perspective, were absent here. A single edifice? A group? A city? Or simply a place? The outline varied each time that it fell upon my retina. Now faint and misty sheets drifted slowly between us, twisting, as if long strands of gauze were buoyed by heated air. The mandala ceased its turning when it had exactly reversed itself. The colors were behind me now, and imperceptible unless I turned my head, an action I had no desire to take. It was pleasant standing there, staring at the formlessness from which all things eventually emerged. . . . Before the Pattern, even, this thing was. I knew this, dimly but surely, at the very center of my consciousness. I knew this, because I was certain that I had been here before. Child of the man I had become, it seemed that I had been brought here in some distant day—whether by Dad or Dworkin, I could not now recall—and had stood or been held in this place or one very near to it, looking out upon the same scene with, I am certain, a similar lack of comprehension, a similar sense of apprehension. My pleasure was tinged with a nervous excitement, a sense of the forbidden, a feeling of dubious anticipation. Peculiarly, at that moment, there rose in me a longing for the Jewel I had had to abandon in my compost heap on the shadow Earth, the thing Dworkin had made so much of. Could it be that some part of me sought a defense or at least a symbol of resistance against whatever was out there? Probably.

As I continued to stare, fascinated, across the chasm, it was as if my eyes adjusted or the prospect shifted once again, subtly. For now I discerned tiny, ghostly forms moving within that place, like slow-motion meteors along the gauzy strands. I waited, regarding them carefully, courting some small understanding of the actions in which they were engaged. At length, one of the strands drifted very near. Shortly thereafter I had my answer.

There was a movement. One of the rushing forms grew larger, and I realized that it was following the twisting way that led toward me. In only a few moments, it took on the proportions of a horseman. As it came on, it assumed a semblance of solidity without losing that ghostly quality which seemed to cling to everything which lay before me. A moment later, I beheld a naked rider on a hairless horse, both deathly pale, rushing in my direction. The rider brandished a bone-white blade; his eyes and the eyes of the horse both flashed red. I did not really know whether he saw me, whether we existed on the same plane of reality, so unnatural was his mien. Yet I unsheathed Grayswandir and took a step backward as he approached.

His long white hair shed tiny sparkling motes, and when he turned his head I knew that he was coming for me, for then I felt his gaze like a cold pressure across the front of my body. I turned sidewise and raised my blade to guard.

He continued, and I realized that both he and the horse were big, bigger even than I had thought. They came on. When they reached the point nearest me—some ten meters, perhaps—the horse reared as the rider drew it to a halt. They regarded me then, bobbing and swaying as if on a raft in a gently swelling sea.

"Your name!" the rider demanded. "Give me your name, who comes to this place!"

His voice produced a crackling sensation in my ears. It was all of one sound level, loud and without inflection.

I shook my head.

"I give my name when I choose, not when I am ordered to," I said. "Who are you?"

He gave three short barks, which I took to be a laugh.

"I will hale you down and about, where you will cry it out forever."

I pointed Grayswandir at his eyes.

"Talk is cheap," I said. "Whisky costs money."

I felt a faint cool sensation just then, as if someone were toying with my Trump, thinking of me. But it was dim, weak, and I had no attention to spare, for the rider had passed some signal to his mount and the beast reared. The distance is too great, I decided. But this thought belonged to another shadow. The beast plunged ahead toward me, departing the tenuous roadway that had been its course.

Its leap bore it to a point far short of my position. But it did not fall from there and vanish, as I had hoped. It resumed the motions of galloping, and although its progress was not fully commensurate with the action, it continued to advance across the abyss at about half-speed.

While this was occurring, I saw that in the distance from which it had come another figure appeared to be headed my way. Nothing to do but stand my ground, fight, and hope that I could dispatch this attacker before the other was upon me.

As the rider advanced, his ruddy gaze flicked over my person and halted when it fell upon Grayswandir. Whatever the nature of the mad illumination at my back, it had tricked the delicate tracery on my blade to life once more, so that that portion of the Pattern it bore swam and sparkled along its length. The horseman was very near by then, but he drew back on the reins and his eyes leaped upward, meeting my own. His nasty grin vanished.

"I know you!" he said. "You are the one called Corwin!"

But we had him, me and my ally momentum.

His mount's front hoofs fell upon the ledge and I rushed forward. The beast's reflexes caused it to seek equal footing for its hind legs despite the drawn reins. The rider swung his blade into a guard position as I came on, but I cross-stepped and attacked from his left. As he moved his blade cross-body, I was already lunging. Grayswandir sheared through his pale hide, entering beneath the sternum and above the guts.

I wrenched my blade free and gouts of fire poured like blood from his wound. His sword arm sagged and his mount uttered a shriek that was almost a whistle as the blazing stream fell upon its neck. I danced back as the rider slumped forward and the beast, now fully footed, plunged on toward me, kicking. I cut again, reflexively, defensively. My blade nicked its left fore-leg, and it, too, began to burn.

I side-stepped once again as it turned and made for me a second time. At that moment, the rider erupted into a pillar of light. The beast bellowed, wheeled, and rushed away. Without pausing, it plunged over the edge and vanished into the abyss, leaving me with the memory of the smoldering head of a cat which had addressed me long ago and the chill which always accompanied the recollection.

I was backed against rock, panting. The wispy road had drifted nearer—ten feet, perhaps, from the ledge. I had developed a cramp in my left side. The second rider was rapidly approaching. He was not pale like the first. His hair was dark and there was color in his face. His mount was a properly maned sorrel. He bore a cocked and bolted crossbow. I glanced behind me and there was no retreat, no crevice into which I might back.

I wiped my palm on my trousers and gripped Grayswandir by the forte of the blade. I turned sideways, so as to present the narrowest target possible. I raised my blade between us, hilt level with my head, point toward the ground, the only shield I possessed.

The rider came abreast of me and halted at the nearest point on the gauzy strip. He raised the crossbow slowly, knowing that if he did not drop me instantly with his single shot, I might be able to hurl my blade like a spear. Our eyes met.

He was beardless, slim. Possibly light-eyed within the squint of his aim. He managed his mount well, with just the pressure of his legs. His hands were big, steady. Capable. A peculiar feeling passed over me as I beheld him.

The moment stretched beyond the point of action. He rocked backward and lowered the weapon slightly, though none of the tension left his stance.

"You," he called out. "Is that the blade Grayswandir?"

"Yes," I answered, "it is."

He continued his appraisal, and something within me looked for words to wear, failed, ran naked away through the night.

"What do you want here?" he asked.

"To depart," I said.

There was a *chish-chá,* as his bolt struck the rock far ahead and to the left of me.

"Go then," he said. "This is a dangerous place for you."

He turned his mount back in the direction from which he had come.

I lowered Grayswandir.

"I won't forget you," I said.

"No," he answered. "Do not."

Then he galloped away, and moments later the gauze drifted off also.

I resheathed Grayswandir and took a step forward. The world was beginning to turn about me again, the light advancing on my right, the dark retreating to my left. I looked about for some way to scale the rocky prominence at my back. It seemed to rise only thirty or forty feet higher, and I wanted the view that might be available from its summit. My ledge extended to both my right and my left. On inspection, the way to the right narrowed quickly, however, without affording a suitable ascent. I turned and made my way to the left.

I came upon a rougher spot in a narrow place beyond a rocky shoulder. Running my gaze up its height, an ascent seemed possible. I checked behind me after the approach of additional threats. The ghostly roadway had drifted farther away; no new riders advanced. I commenced climbing.

The going was not difficult, though the height proved greater than it had seemed from below. Likely a symptom of the spatial distortion which seemed to have affected my sight of so much else in this place. After a time, I hauled myself up and stood erect at a point which afforded a better view in the direction opposite the abyss.

Once again, I beheld the chaotic colors. From my right, the darkness herded them. The land they danced above was rock-cropped and cratered, no sign of any life within it. Passing through its midst, however, from the far horizon to a point in the mountains somewhere to the right, inky and serpentine, ran what could only be the black road.

Another ten minutes of climbing and maneuvering, and I had positioned myself to view its terminus. It swept through a broad pass in the mountains and ran right to the very edge of the abyss. There, its blackness merged with that which filled the place, noticeable now only by virtue of the fact that no stars shone through it. Using this occlusion to gauge it, I obtained the impression that it continued on to the dark eminence about which the misty strips drifted.

I stretched out on my belly, so as to disturb the outline of the low crest as little as possible to whatever unseen eyes might flick across it. Lying there, I thought upon the opening of this way. The damage to the Pattern had laid Amber open to this access, and I believed that my curse had provided the precipitating element. I felt now that it would have come to pass without me, but I was certain that I had done my part. The guilt was still partly mine though no longer entirely so, as I had once believed. I thought then of Eric, as he lay dying on Kolvir. He had said that as much as he hated me, he was saving his dying curse for the enemies of Amber. In other words, this, and these. Ironic. My efforts were now entirely directed toward making good on my least-liked brother's dying wish. His curse to cancel my curse, me as the agent. Fitting though, perhaps, in some larger sense.

I sought, and was pleased not to discover, ranks of glowing riders setting forth or assembling upon that road. Unless another raiding party was already under way Amber was still temporarily safe. A number of things immediately troubled me, however. Mainly, if time did indeed behave as peculiarly in that place as Dara's possible origin indicated, then why had there not been another attack? They had certainly had ample time in which to recover and prepare for another assault. Had something occurred recently, by Amber's time, that is, to alter the nature of their strategy? If so, what? My weapons? Brand's recovery? Or something else? I wondered, too, how far Benedict's outposts reached. Certainly not this far, or I should have been informed. Had he ever been to this place? Had any of the others, within recent memory, stood where I had just stood, looking upon the Courts of Chaos, knowing something that I did not know? I resolved to question Brand and Benedict in this regard as soon as I returned.

All of which led me to wonder how time was behaving with me, at that moment. Better not to spend any more time here than I had to, I decided. I scanned the other Trumps I had removed from Dworkin's desk. While they were all of them interesting, I was familiar with none of the scenes depicted. I slipped my own case then and riffled through to Random's Trump.

Perhaps he was the one who had tried to contact me earlier. I raised his card and regarded it.

Shortly, it swam before my eyes and I looked upon a blurred kaleidoscope of images, the impression of Random in their midst. Motion, and twisting perspectives . . .

"Random," I said. "This is Corwin."

I felt his mind, but there was no response from it. It struck me then that he was in the middle of a hellride, all his concentration bent on wrapping the stuff of Shadow about him. He could not respond without losing control. I blocked the Trump with my hand, breaking the contact.

I cut to Gèrard's card. Moments later, there was contact. I stood.

"Corwin, where are you?" he inquired.

"At the end of the world," I said. "I want to come home."

"Come ahead."

He extended his hand. I reached out and clasped it, stepped forward.

We were on the ground floor of the palace in Amber, in the sitting room to which we had all adjourned on the night of Brand's return. It seemed to be early morning. There was a fire going on the grate. No one else was present.

"I tried to reach you earlier," he said. "I think Brand did, too. But I can't be sure."

"How long have I been away?"

"Eight days," he said.

"Glad I hurried. What's happening?"

"Nothing untoward," he said. "I do not know what Brand wants. He kept asking for you, and I could not reach you. Finally, I gave him a deck and told him to see whether he could do any better. Apparently, he could not."

"I was distracted," I said, "and the time-flow differential was bad."

He nodded.

"I have been avoiding him now that he is out of

danger. He is in one of his black moods again, and he insists he can take care of himself. He is right, in that, and it is just as well."

"Where is he now?"

"Back in his own quarters, and he was still there as of perhaps an hour ago—brooding."

"Has he been out at all?"

"A few brief walks. But not for the past several days."

"I guess I had best go see him then. Any word on Random?"

"Yes," he said. "Benedict returned several days ago. He said they had found a number of leads concerning Random's son. He helped him check on a couple of them. One led further, but Benedict felt he had best not be away from Amber for too long, things being as uncertain as they are. So he left Random to continue the search on his own. He gained something in the venture, though. He came back sporting an artificial arm—a beautiful piece of work. He can do anything with it that he could before."

"Really?" I said. "It sounds strangely familiar."

He smiled, nodded.

"He told me you had brought it back for him from Tir-na Nog'th. In fact, he wants to speak with you about it as soon as possible."

"I'll bet," I said. "Where is he now?"

"At one of the outposts he has established along the black road. You would have to reach him by Trump."

"Thanks," I said. "Anything further on Julian or Fiona?"

He shook his head.

"All right," I said, turning toward the door. "I guess I will go see Brand first."

"I am curious to know what it is that he wants," he said.

"I will remember that," I told him.

I left the room and headed for the stairs.

7.

I rapped on Brand's door.

"Come in, Corwin," he said.

I did, deciding as I crossed the threshold that I would not ask him how he had known who it was. His room was a gloomy place, candles burning despite the fact that it was daytime and he had four windows. The shutters were closed on three of them. The fourth was only part way open. Brand stood beside this one, staring out toward the sea. He was dressed all in black velvet with a silver chain about his neck. His belt was also of silver—a fine, linked affair. He played with a small dagger, and did not look at me as I entered. He was still pale, but his beard was neatly trimmed and he looked well scrubbed and a bit heavier than he had when last I had seen him.

"You are looking better," I said. "How are you feeling?"

He turned and regarded me, expressionless, his eyes half-closed.

"Where the hell have you been?" he said.

"Hither and yon. What did you want to see me about?"

"I asked you where you've been."

"And I heard you," I said, reopening the door behind me. "Now I am going to go out and come back in. Supposing we start this conversation over again?"

He sighed.

"Wait a minute. I am sorry," he said. "Why are we

all so thin-skinned? I do not know. . . . All right. It may be better if I do start over again."

He sheathed his dagger and crossed to sit in a heavy chair of black wood and leather.

"I got to worrying about all the things we had discussed," he said, "and some that we had not. I waited what seemed an appropriate time for you to have concluded your business in Tir-na Nog'th and returned. I then inquired after you and was told you had not yet come back. I waited longer. First I was impatient, and then I grew concerned that you might have been ambushed by our enemies. When I inquired again later, I learned that you had been back only long enough to speak with Random's wife—it must have been a conversation of great moment—and then to take a nap. You then departed once more. I was irritated that you had not seen fit to keep me posted as to events, but I resolved to wait a bit longer. Finally, I asked Gérard to get hold of you with your Trump. When he failed, I was quite concerned. I tried it myself then, and while it seemed that I touched you on several occasions I could not get through. I feared for you, and now I see that I had nothing to fear all along. Hence, I was abrupt."

"I see," I said, taking a seat off to his right. "Actually, time was running faster for me than it was for you, so from where I am sitting I have hardly been away. You are probably further recuperated from your puncture than I am from mine."

He smiled faintly and nodded.

"That is something, anyway," he said, "for my pains."

"I have had a few pains myself," I said, "so don't give me any more. You wanted me for something. Let's have it."

"Something is bothering you," he said. "Perhaps we ought to discuss that first."

"All right," I said. "Let's."

I turned and looked at the painting on the wall beside the door. An oil, a rather somber rendering of the well at Mirata, two men standing beside their horses nearby, talking.

"You've a distinctive style," I said.

"In all things," he replied.

"You stole my next sentence," I said, locating Martin's Trump and passing it to him.

He remained expressionless as he examined it, gave me one brief, sidelong look and then nodded.

"I cannot deny my hand," he said.

"It executed more than that card, your hand. Didn't it?"

He traced his upper lip with the tip of his tongue.

"Where did you find it?" he asked.

"Right where you left it, at the heart of things—in the real Amber."

"So . . ." he said, rising from the chair and returning to the window, holding up the card as if to study it in a better light. "So," he repeated, "you are aware of more than I had guessed. How did you learn of the primal Pattern?"

I shook my head.

"You answer my question first: Did you stab Martin?"

He turned toward me once again, stared a moment, then nodded sharply. His eyes continued to search my face.

"Why?" I asked.

"Someone had to," he explained, "to open the way for the powers we needed. We drew straws."

"And you won."

"Won? Lost?" He shrugged. "What does any of this matter now? Things did not come about as we had intended. I am a different person now than I was then."

"Did you kill him?"

"What?"

"Martin, Random's son. Did he die as a result of the wound you inflicted?"

He turned his hands palms upward.

"I do not know," he said. "If he did not, it was not because I did not try. You need look no further.

You have found your guilty party. Now that you have, what are you going to do?"

I shook my head.

"I? Nothing. For all I know, the lad may still be living."

"Then let us move on to matters of greater moment. For how long have you known of the existence of the true Pattern?"

"Long enough," I said. "Its origin, its functions, the effect of the blood of Amber upon it—long enough. I paid more attention to Dworkin than you might have thought. I saw no gain to be had in damaging the fabric of existence, though. So I let Rover lie sleeping for a long, long while. It did not even occur to me until I spoke with you recently that the black road might have been connected with such foolishness. When I went to inspect the Pattern I found Martin's Trump and all the rest."

"I was not aware that you were acquainted with Martin."

"I have never set eyes on him."

"Then how were you aware he was the subject of the Trump?"

"I was not alone in that place."

"Who was with you?"

I smiled.

"No, Brand. It is still your turn. You told me when last we talked that the enemies of Amber hied all the way from the Courts of Chaos, that they have access to the realm via the black road because of something you and Bleys and Fiona had done back when you were of one mind as to the best way to take the throne. Now I know what it is that you did. Yet Benedict has been watching the black road and I have just looked upon the Courts of Chaos. There is no new massing of forces, no movement toward us upon that road. I know that time flows differently in that place. They should have had more than enough time to ready a new assault. I want to know what is holding them back.

Why have they not moved? What are they waiting for, Brand?"

"You credit me with more knowledge than I possess."

"I don't think so. You are the resident expert on the subject. You have dealt with them. That Trump is evidence that you have been holding back on other matters. Don't weasel, just talk."

"The Courts . . ." he said. "You have been busy. Eric was a fool not to have killed you immediately— if he was aware you had knowledge of these things."

"Eric was a fool," I acknowledged. "You are not. Now talk."

"But I am a fool," he said, "a sentimental one, at that. Do you recall the day of our last argument, here in Amber, so long ago?"

"Somewhat."

"I was sitting on the edge of my bed. You were standing by my writing desk. As you turned away and headed toward the door, I resolved to kill you. I reached beneath my bed, where I keep a cocked crossbow with a bolt in it. I actually had my hand on it and was about to raise it when I realized something which stopped me."

He paused.

"What was that?" I asked.

"Look over there by the door."

I looked, I saw nothing special. I began to shake my head, just as he said, "On the floor."

Then I realized what it was—russet and olive and brown and green, with a small geometric pattern.

He nodded.

"You were standing on my favorite rug. I did not want to get blood on it. Later, my anger passed. So I, too, am a victim of emotion and circumstance."

"Lovely story—" I began.

"—but now you want me to stop stalling. I was not stalling, however. I was attempting to make a point. We are all of us alive by one another's sufferance and an occasional fortunate accident. I am going to propose suspending that sufferance and eliminating the possibility of accident in a couple of very important cases. First though, to answer your question, while I do not know for certain what is holding them back, I can venture a very good guess. Bleys has assembled a large strike force for an attack on Amber. It will be nowhere near the scale of the one on which you accompanied him, however. You see, he will be counting on the memory of that last attack to have conditioned the response to this one. It will probably also be preceded by attempts to assassinate Benedict and yourself. The entire affair will be a feint, though. I would guess that Fiona has contacted the Courts of Chaos—may even be there right now—and has prepared them for the real attack, which might be expected any time after Bleys's diversionary foray. Therefore—"

"You say this is a very good guess," I interrupted. "But we do not even know for certain that Bleys is still living."

"Bleys is alive," he said. "I was able to ascertain his existence via his Trump—even a brief assessment of his current activities—before he became aware of my presence and blocked me out. He is very sensitive to such surveillance. I found him in the field with troops he intends to employ against Amber."

"And Fiona?"

"No," he said, "I did no experimenting with her Trump, and I would advise you not to either. She is extremely dangerous, and I did not want to lay my self open to her influence. My estimate of her current situation is based on deduction rather than direct knowledge. I would be willing to rely on it, though."

"I see," I said.

"I have a plan."

"Go ahead."

"The manner in which you retrieved me from durance was quite inspired, combining the forces of everyone's concentration as you did. The same principle could be utilized again, to a different end. A force such as that would break through a person's defense

93

fairly easily—even someone like Fiona, if the effort is properly directed."

"That is to say, directed by yourself?"

"Of course. I propose that we assemble the family and force our way through to Bleys and Fiona, wherever they may be. We hold them, locked in the full, in the flesh, just for a moment or so. Just long enough for me to strike."

"As you did Martin?"

"Better, I trust. Martin was able to break free at the last moment. That should not occur this time, with all of you helping. Even three or four would probably be sufficient."

"You really think you can pull it off that easily?"

"I know we had better try. Time is running. You will be one of the ones executed when they take Amber. So will I. What do you say?"

"If I become convinced that it is necessary. Then I would have no choice but to go along with it."

"It is necessary, believe me. The next thing is that I will need the Jewel of Judgment."

"What for?"

"If Fiona is truly in the Courts of Chaos, the Trump alone will probably be insufficient to reach her and hold her—even with all of us behind it. In her case, I will require the Jewel to focus our energies."

"I suppose that could be arranged."

"Then the sooner we are about it the better. Can you set things up for tonight? I am sufficiently recovered to handle my end of it."

"Hell, no," I said, standing.

"What do you mean?" He clenched the arms of the chair, half-rising. "Why not?"

"I said I would go along with it if I became convinced that it was necessary. You have admitted that a lot of this is conjecture. That alone is sufficient to keep me from being convinced."

"Forget about being convinced then. Can you afford to take the chance? The next attack is going to be a lot stronger than the last, Corwin. They are aware of your new weapons. They are going to allow for this in their planning."

"Even if I agreed with you, Brand, I am certain I could not convince the others that the executions are necessary."

"Convince them? Just tell them! You've got them all by the throat, Corwin! You are on top right now. You want to stay there, don't you?"

I smiled and moved toward the door.

"I will, too," I said, "by doing things my way. I will keep your suggestion on file."

"Your way is going to get you dead. Sooner than you think."

"I am standing on your rug again," I said.

He laughed.

"Very good. But I was not threatening you. You know what I meant. You are responsible for all of Amber now. You have to do the right thing."

"And you know what I meant. I am not going to kill a couple more of us because of your suspicions. I would need more than that."

"When you get it, it may be too late."

I shrugged.

"We'll see."

I reached toward the door.

"What are you going to do now?"

I shook my head.

"I don't tell anybody everything that I know, Brand. It is a kind of insurance."

"I can appreciate that. I only hope that you know enough."

"Or perhaps you fear that I know too much," I said.

For a moment a wary look danced on the muscles beneath his eyes. Then he smiled.

"I am not afraid of you, brother," he said.

"It is good to have nothing to fear," I said.

I opened the door.

"Wait," he said.

"Yes?"

"You neglected to tell me who was with you when you discovered Martin's Trump, in the place where I had left it."

"Why, it was Random," I said.

"Oh. Is he aware of the particulars?"

"If you mean, does he know that you stabbed his son," I said, "the answer is no, not yet."

"I see. And of Benedict's new arm? I understand that you somehow got it for him in Tir-na Nog'th. I would like to know more about this."

"Not now," I said. "Let's save something for our next get-together. It won't be all that long."

I went on out and closed the door, my silent regards to the rug.

3.

After visiting the kitchens, compiling an enormous meal and demolishing it, I headed for the stables, where I located a handsome young sorrel which had once belonged to Eric. I made friends with him in spite of this, and a short while later we were moving toward the trail down Kolvir which would take us to the camp of my Shadow forces. As I rode and digested, I tried to sort out the events and revelations of what, to me, had been the past few hours. If Amber had indeed arisen as the result of Dworkin's act of rebellion within the Courts of Chaos, then it followed that we were all of us related to the very forces which now threatened us. It was, of course, difficult to decide how far anything Dworkin said might now be trusted. Yet, the black road did run to the Courts of Chaos, apparently as a direct result of Brand's ritual, a thing which he had based on principles learned from Dworkin. Fortunately, for now, the parts of Dworkin's narrative which required the greatest credulity were those things which were not of any great moment, from an immediate, practical standpoint. Still, I had mixed feelings about being descended from a unicorn—

"Corwin!"

I drew rein. I opened my mind to the sending and the image of Ganelon appeared.

"I am here," I said. "Where did you get hold of a set of Trumps? And learn how to use them?"

"I picked up a pack from the case in the library

a while back. Thought it a good idea to have a way of getting in touch with you in a hurry. As for using them, I just did what you and the others seem to do—study the Trump, think about it, concentrate on getting in touch with the person."

"I should have gotten you a pack long ago," I said. "It was an oversight on my part which I am glad you've remedied. Are you just testing them now, or did something come up?"

"Something," he said. "Where are you?"

"As chance would have it, I am on my way down to see you."

"You are all right?"

"Yes."

"Fine. Come ahead then. I'd rather not try bringing you through this thing, the way you people do. It is not that urgent. I will see you by and by."

"Yes."

He broke the contact and I rustled the reins and continued on. For a moment, I had been irritated that he had not simply asked me for a deck. Then I recalled that I had been away for over a week, by Amber's time. He had probably been getting worried, didn't trust any of the others to do it for him. Perhaps rightly so.

The descent went quickly, as did the balance of the journey to the camp. The horse—whose name, by the way, was Drum—seemed happy to be going somewhere and had a tendency to pull away at the least excuse. I gave him his head at one point to tire him a bit, and it was not too long afterward that I sighted the camp. I realized at about that time that I missed Star.

I was the subject of stares and salutes as I rode into camp. A silence followed me and all activity ceased as I passed. I wondered whether they believed I had come to deliver a battle order.

Ganelon emerged from his tent before I had dismounted.

98

"Fast," he observed, clasping my hand as I came down. "Pretty horse, that."

"Yes," I agreed, turning the reins over to his orderly. "What news have you?"

"Well . . ." he said. "I've been talking to Benedict . . ."

"Something stirring on the black road?"

"No, no. Nothing like that. He came to see me after he returned from those friends of his—the Tecys —to tell me that Random was all right, that he was following a lead as to Martin's whereabouts. We got to talking of other matters after that, and finally he asked me to tell him everything I knew about Dara. Random had told him about her walking the Pattern, and he had decided then that too many people other than yourself were aware of her existence."

"So what did you tell him?"

"Everything."

"Including the guesswork, the speculation after Tir-na Nog'th?"

"Just so."

"I see. How did he take this?"

"He seemed excited about it. Happy, I'd even say. Come talk with him yourself."

I nodded and he turned toward his tent. He pushed back the flap and stepped aside. I entered.

Benedict was seated on a low stool beside a foot locker atop which a map had been spread. He was tracing something on the map with the long metal finger of the glinting, skeletal hand attached to the deadly, silver-cabled, firepinned mechanical arm I had brought back from the city in the sky, the entire device now attached to the stump of his right arm a little below the point where the sleeve had been cut away from his brown shirt, a transformation which halted me with a momentary shudder, so much did he resemble the ghost I had encountered. His eyes rose to meet my own and he raised the hand in greeting, a casual, perfectly executed gesture, and he smiled the broadest smile I had ever seen crease his face.

"Corwin!" he said, and then he rose and extended that hand.

I had to force myself to clasp the device which had almost killed me. But Benedict looked more kindly disposed toward me than he had in a long while. I shook the new hand and its pressures were perfect. I tried to disregard its coldness and angularity and almost succeeded, in my amazement at the control he had acquired over it in such a brief time.

"I owe you an apology," he said. "I have wronged you. I am very sorry."

"It's all right," I said. "I understand."

He clasped me for a moment, and my belief that things had apparently been set right between us was darkened only by the grip of those precise and deadly fingers on my shoulder.

Ganelon chuckled and brought up another stool, which he set at the other end of the locker. My irritation at his having aired the subject I had not wanted mentioned, whatever the circumstances, was submerged by the sight of its effects. I could not remember having seen Benedict in better spirits; Ganelon was obviously pleased at having effected the resolution of our differences.

I smiled myself and accepted a seat, unbuckling my sword belt and hanging Grayswandir on the tent pole. Ganelon produced three glasses and a bottle of wine. As he set the glasses before us and poured, he remarked, "To return the hospitality of your tent, that night, back in Avalon."

Benedict took up his glass with but the faintest of clicks.

"There is more ease in this tent," he said. "Is that not so, Corwin?"

I nodded and raised my glass.

"To that ease. May it always prevail."

"I have had my first opportunity in a long while," he said, "to talk with Random at some length. He has changed quite a bit."

"Yes," I agreed.

"I am more inclined to trust him now than I was in days gone by. We had the time to talk after we left the Tecys."

"Where were you headed?"

"Some comments Martin had made to his host seemed to indicate that he was going to a place I knew of further off in Shadow—the block city of Heerat. We journeyed there and found this to be correct. He had passed that way."

"I am not familiar with Heerat," I said.

"A place of adobe and stone—a commercial center at the junction of several trade routes. There, Random found news which took him eastward and probably deeper into Shadow. We parted company at Heerat, for I did not want to be away from Amber overlong. Also, there was a personal matter I was anxious to pursue. He told me how he had seen Dara walk the Pattern on the day of the battle."

"That's right," I said. "She did. I was there, too."

He nodded.

"As I said, Random had impressed me. I was inclined to believe he was telling the truth. If this were so, then it was possible that you were also. Granting this, I had to pursue the matter of the girl's allegations. You were not available, so I came to Ganelon—this was several days ago—and had him tell me everything he knew about Dara."

I glanced at Ganelon, who inclined his head slightly.

"So you now believe you have uncovered a new relative," I said, "a mendacious one, to be sure, and quite possibly an enemy—but a relative, nevertheless. What is your next move?"

He took a sip of wine.

"I would like to believe in the relationship," he said. "The notion somehow pleases me. So I would like to establish it or negate it to a certainty. If it turns out that we are indeed related, then I would like to understand the motives behind her actions. And I would like to learn why she never made her existence known to me directly." He put down his glass, raised his new hand and flexed the fingers. "So I would like to begin," he continued, "by learning of those things you experienced in Tir-na Nog'th which apply to me and to Dara. I am also extremely curious about this hand, which behaves as if it were made for me. I have never heard of a physical object being obtained in the city in the sky." He made a fist, unclenched it, rotated the wrist, extended the arm, raised it, lowered it gently to his knee. "Random performed a very effective piece of surgery, don't you think?" he concluded.

"Very," I agreed.

"So, will you tell me the story?"

I nodded and took a sip of my wine.

"It was in the palace in the sky that it occurred," I said. "The place was filled with inky, shifting shadows. I felt impelled to visit the throne room. I did this, and when the shadows moved aside, I saw you standing to the right of the throne, wearing that arm. When things cleared further, I saw Dara seated upon the throne. I advanced and touched her with Grayswandir, which made me visible to her. She declared me dead these several centuries and bade me return to my grave. When I demanded her lineage, she said she was descended of you and of the hellmaid Lintra."

Benedict drew a deep breath but said nothing. I continued:

"Time, she said, moved at such a different rate in the place of her birth, that several generations had passed there. She was the first of them possessed of regular human attributes. She again bade me depart. During this time, you had been studying Grayswandir. You struck then to remove her from danger, and we fought. My blade could reach you and your hand could reach me. That was all. Otherwise, it was a confrontation of ghosts. As the sun began to rise and the city to fade, you had me in a grip with that hand. I struck it free of the arm with Grayswandir and escaped. It was returned with me because it was still clasping my shoulder."

"Curious," Benedict said. "I have known that place to render false prophecies—the fears and hidden desires of the visitor, rather than a true picture of what is to be. But then, it often reveals unknown truths as well. And as in most other things, it is difficult to separate the valid from the spurious. How did you read it?"

"Benedict," I said, "I am inclined to believe the story of her origin. You have never seen her, but I have. She does resemble you in some ways. As for the rest . . . it is doubtless as you said—that which is left after the truth has been separated out."

He nodded slowly, and I could tell that he was not convinced but did not want to push the matter. He knew as well as I did what the rest implied. If he were to pursue his claim to the throne and succeed in achieving it, it was possible that he might one day step aside in favor of his only descendant.

"What are you going to do?" I asked him.

"Do?" he said. "What is Random now doing about Martin? I shall seek her, find her, have the story from her own lips, and then decide for myself. This will have to wait, however, until the matter of the black road is settled. That is another matter I wish to discuss with you."

"Yes?"

"If time moves so differently in their stronghold, they have had more than they need in which to mount another attack. I do not want to keep waiting to meet them in indecisive encounters. I am contemplating following the black road back to its source and attacking them on their home ground. I would like to do it with your concurrence."

"Benedict," I said, "have you ever looked upon the Courts of Chaos?"

He raised his head and stared at the blank wall of the tent.

"Ages ago, when I was young," he said, "I hellrode as far as I might go, to the end of everything. There, beneath a divided sky, I looked upon an awesome

103

abyss. I do not know if the place lies there or if the road runs that far, but I am prepared to take that way again, if such is the case."

"Such is the case," I said.

"How can you be certain?"

"I am just returned from that land. A dark citadel hovers within it. The road goes to it."

"How difficult was the way?"

"Here," I said, taking out the Trump and passing it to him. "This was Dworkin's. I found it among his things. I only just tried it. It took me there. Time is already rapid at that point. I was attacked by a rider on a drifting roadway, of a sort not shown on the card. Trump contact is difficult there, perhaps because of the time differential. Gérard brought me back."

He studied the card.

"It seems the place I saw that time," he said at length. "This solves our logistics problems. With one of us on either end of a Trump connection we can transport the troops right through, as we did that day from Kolvir to Garnath."

I nodded.

"That is one of the reasons I showed it to you, to indicate my good faith. There may be another way, involving less risk than running our forces into the unknown. I want you to hold off on this venture until I have explored my way further."

"I will have to hold off in any event, to obtain some intelligence concerning that place. We do not even know whether your automatic weapons will function there, do we?"

"No, I did not have one along to test."

He pursed his lips.

"You really should have thought to take one and try it."

"The circumstances of my departure did not permit this."

"Circumstances?"

"Another time. It is not relevant here. You spoke of following the black road to its source . . ."

"Yes?"

"That is not its true source. Its real source lies in the true Amber, in the defect in the primal Pattern."

"Yes, I understand that. Both Random and Ganelon have described your journey to the place of the true Pattern, and the damage you discovered there. I see the analogy, the possible connection—"

"Do you recall my flight from Avalon, and your pursuit?"

In answer, he only smiled faintly.

"There was a point where we crossed the black road," I said. "Do you recall it?"

He narrowed his eyes.

"Yes," he said. "You cut a path through it. The world had returned to normal at that point. I had forgotten."

"It was an effect of the Pattern upon it," I said, "one which I believe can be employed upon a much larger scale."

"How much larger?"

"To wipe out the entire thing."

He leaned back and studied my face.

"Then why are you not about it?"

"There are a few preliminaries I must undertake."

"How much time will they involve?"

"Not too much. Possibly as little as a few days. Perhaps a few weeks."

"Why didn't you mention all of this sooner?"

"I only learned how to go about it recently."

"How *do* you go about it?"

"Basically, it amounts to repairing the Pattern."

"All right," he said. "Say you succeed. The enemy will still be out there." He gestured toward Garnath and the black road. "Someone gave them passage once."

"The enemy has always been out there," I said. "And it will be up to us to see that they are not given passage again—by dealing properly with those who provided it in the first place."

"I go along with you on that," he said, "but that

105

is not what I meant. They require a lesson, Corwin. I want to teach them a proper respect for Amber, such a respect that even if the way is opened again they will fear to use it. That is what I meant. It is necessary."

"You do not know what it would be like to carry a battle to that place, Benedict. It is—literally—indescribable."

He smiled and stood.

"Then I guess I had best go see for myself," he said. "I will keep this card for a time, if you don't mind."

"I don't mind."

"Good. Then you be on with your business about the Pattern, Corwin, and I will be about my own. This will take me some time, too. I must go give my commanders orders concerning my absence now. Let us agree that neither of us commence anything of a final nature without checking first with the other."

"Agreed," I said.

We finished our wine.

"I will be under way myself, very soon now," I said. "So, good luck."

"To you, also." He smiled again. "Things are better," he said, and he clasped my shoulder as he passed to the entrance.

We followed him outside.

"Bring Benedict's horse," Ganelon directed the orderly who stood beneath a nearby tree; and turning, he offered Benedict his hand. "I, too, want to wish you luck," he said.

Benedict nodded and shook his hand.

"Thank you, Ganelon. For many things."

Benedict withdrew his Trumps.

"I can bring Gérard up to date," he said, "before my horse arrives."

He riffled through them, withdrew one, studied it.

"How do you go about repairing the Pattern?" Ganelon asked me.

"I have to get hold of the Jewel of Judgment again," I said. "With it, I can reinscribe the damaged area."

"Is this dangerous?"

"Yes."

"Where is the Jewel?"

"Back on the shadow Earth, where I left it."

"Why did you abandon it?"

"I feared that it was killing me."

He contorted his features into a near-impossible grimace.

"I don't like the sound of this, Corwin. There must be another way."

"If I knew a better way, I'd take it."

"Supposing you just followed Benedict's plan and took them all on? You said yourself that he could raise infinite legions in Shadow. You also said that he is the best man there is in the field."

"Yet the damage would remain in the Pattern, and something else would come to fill it. Always. The enemy of the moment is not as important as our own inner weakness. If this is not mended we are already defeated, though no foreign conqueror stands within our walls."

He turned away.

"I cannot argue with you. You know your own realm," he said. "But I still feel you may be making a grave mistake by risking yourself on what may prove unnecessary at a time when you are very much needed."

I chuckled, for it was Vialle's word and I had not wanted to call it my own when she had said it.

"It is my duty," I told him.

He did not reply.

Benedict, a dozen paces away, had apparently reached Gérard, for he would mutter something, then pause and listen. We stood there, waiting for him to conclude his conversation so that we could see him off.

". . . Yes, he is here now," I heard him say. "No, I doubt that very much. But—"

Benedict glanced at me several times and shook his head.

107

"No, I do not think so," he said. Then, "All right, come ahead."

He extended his new hand, and Gérard stepped into being, clasping it. Gérard turned his head, saw me, and immediately moved in my direction.

He ran his eyes up and down and back and forth across my entire person, as if searching for something.

"What is the matter?" I said.

"Brand," he replied. "He is no longer in his quarters. At least, most of him isn't. He left some blood behind. The place is also broken up enough to show there had been a fight."

I glanced down at my shirt front and trousers.

"And you are looking for bloodstains? As you can see, these are the same things I had on earlier. They may be dirty and wrinkled, but that's all."

"That does not really prove anything," he said.

"It was your idea to look. Not mine. What makes you think I—"

"You were the last one to see him," he said.

"Except for the person he had a fight with—if he really did."

"What do you mean by that?"

"You know his temper, his moods. We had a small argument. He might have started breaking things up after I left, maybe cut himself, gotten disgusted, trumped out for a change of scene— Wait! His rug! Was there any blood on that small, fancy rug before his door?"

"I am not sure—no, I don't think so. Why?"

"Circumstantial evidence that he did it himself. He was very fond of that rug. He avoided messing it."

"I don't buy it," Gérard said, "and Caine's death still looks peculiar—and Benedict's servants, who could have found out you wanted gunpowder. Now Brand—"

"This could well be another attempt to frame me," I said, "and Benedict and I have come to better terms."

He turned toward Benedict, who had not moved

from where he stood a dozen paces away, regarding us without expression, listening.

"Has he explained away those deaths?" Gérard asked him.

"Not directly," Benedict answered, "but much of the rest of the story now stands in a better light. So much so, that I am inclined to believe all of it."

Gérard shook his head and glared down at me again.

"Still unsettled," he said. "What were you and Brand arguing about?"

"Gérard," I said, "that is our business, till Brand and I decide otherwise."

"I dragged him back to life and watched over him, Corwin. I didn't do it just to see him killed in a squabble."

"Use your brains," I told him. "Whose idea was it to search for him the way that we did? To bring him back?"

"You wanted something from him," he said. "You finally got it. Then he became an impediment."

"No. But even if that were the case, do you think I would be so damned obvious about it? If he has been killed, then it is on the same order as Caine's death—an attempt to frame me."

"You used the obviousness excuse with Caine, too. It seems to me it could be a kind of subtlety—a thing you are good at."

"We have been through this before, Gérard . . ."

". . . And you know what I told you then."

"It would be difficult to have forgotten."

He reached forward and seized my right shoulder. I immediately drove my left hand into his stomach and pulled away. It occurred to me then that perhaps I should have told him what Brand and I had been talking about. But I didn't like the way he had asked me.

He came at me again. I side-stepped and caught him with a light left near the right eye. I kept jabbing after that, mainly to keep his head back. I was in no real shape to fight him again, and Grayswandir was back in the tent. I had no other weapon with me.

I kept circling him. My side hurt if I kicked with my left leg. I caught him once on the thigh with my right, but I was slow and off-balance and could not really follow through. I continued to jab.

Finally, he blocked my left and managed to drop his hand on my biceps. I should have pulled away then, but he was open. I stepped in with a heavy right to his stomach, all of my strength behind it. It bent him forward with a gasp, but his grip tightened on my arm. He blocked my attempted uppercut with his left, continuing its forward motion until the heel of his hand slammed against my chest, at the same time jerking my left arm backward and to the side with such force that I was thrown to the ground. If he came down on me, that was it.

He dropped to one knee and reached for my throat.

9.

I moved to block his hand, but it halted in midreach. Turning my head, I saw that another hand had fallen upon Gérard's arm, was now grasping it, was holding it back.

I rolled away. When I looked up again, I saw that Ganelon had caught hold of him. Gérard jerked his arm forward, but it did not come free.

"Stay out of this, Ganelon," he said.

"Get going, Corwin!" Ganelon said. "Get the Jewel!"

Even as he called out, Gérard was beginning to rise. Ganelon crossed with his left and connected with Gérard's jaw. Gérard sprawled at his feet. Ganelon moved in and swung a kick toward his kidney, but Gérard caught his foot and heaved him over backward. I scrambled back into a crouch, supporting myself with one hand.

Gérard came up off the ground and rushed Ganelon, who was just recovering his feet. As he was almost upon him, Ganelon came up with a double-fisted blow to Gérard's midsection, which halted him in his tracks. Instantly, Ganelon's fists were moving like pistons against Gérard's abdomen. For several moments, Gérard seemed too dazed to protect himself, and when he finally bent and brought his arms in, Ganelon caught him with a right to the jaw that staggered him backward. Ganelon immediately rushed forward, throwing his arms about Gérard as he slammed into him and hooking his right leg behind Gérard's own. Gérard toppled and Ganelon fell upon him. He straddled Gérard then and drove his right fist against his jaw. When Gérard's head rolled back, Ganelon crossed with his left.

Benedict suddenly moved to intervene, but Ganelon chose that moment to rise to his feet. Gérard lay unconscious, bleeding from his mouth and nose.

I got shakily to my own feet, dusted myself off.

Ganelon grinned at me.

"Don't stay around," he said. "I don't know how I would do in a rematch. Go find the trinket."

I glanced at Benedict and he nodded. I returned to the tent for Grayswandir. When I emerged, Gérard still had not moved, but Benedict stood before me.

"Remember," he said, "you've my Trump and I've yours. Nothing final without a conference."

I nodded. I was going to ask him why he had seemed willing to help Gérard, but not me. But second thoughts had me and I decided against spoiling our fresh-minted amity.

"Okay."

I headed toward the horses. Ganelon clapped me on the shoulder as I came up to him.

"Good luck," he said. "I'd go with you, but I am needed here—especially with Benedict trumping off to Chaos."

"Good show," I said. "I shouldn't have any trouble. Don't worry."

I went off to the paddock. Shortly, I was mounted and moving. Ganelon threw me a salute as I passed and I returned it. Benedict was kneeling beside Gérard.

I headed for the nearest trail into Arden. The sea lay at my back, Garnath and the black road to the left, Kolvir to my right. I had to gain some distance before I could work with the stuff of Shadow. The day lay clean once Garnath was lost to sight, several rises and dips later. I struck the trail and followed its long curve into the wood, where moist shadows and distant bird songs reminded me of the long periods of peace we had known of old and the silken, gleaming presence of the maternal unicorn.

My aches faded into the rhythm of the ride, and I thought once again of the encounter I had departed. It was not difficult to understand Gérard's attitude, since he had already told me of his suspicions and issued me a warning. Still, it was such bad timing for whatever had happened with Brand that I could not but see it as another action intended either to slow me or to stop me entirely. It was fortunate that Ganelon had been on hand, in good shape, and able to put his fists in the right places at the proper times. I wondered what Benedict would have done if there had only been the three of us present. I'd a feeling he would have waited and intervened only at the very last moment, to stop Gérard from killing me. I was still not happy with our accord, though it was certainly an improvement over the previous state of affairs.

All of which made me wonder again what had become of Brand. Had Fiona or Bleys finally gotten to him? Had he attempted his proposed assassinations singlehanded and been met with a counterthrust, then dragged through his intended victim's Trump? Had his old allies from the Courts of Chaos somehow gotten through to him? Had one of his horny-handed guardians from the tower finally been able to reach him? Or had it been as I had suggested to Gérard—an accidental self-injury in a fit of rage, followed by an ill-tempered flight from Amber to do his brooding and plotting elsewhere?

When that many questions arise from a single event the answer is seldom obtainable by pure logic. I had to sort out the possibilities though, to have something to reach for when more facts did turn up. In the meantime, I thought carefully over everything he had told me, regarding his allegations in light of those things which I now knew. With one exception, I did not doubt most of the facts. He had built too cleverly to have the edifice simply toppled—but then, he had had

113

a lot of time to think these things over. No, it was in his manner of presenting events that something had been hidden by misdirection. His recent proposal practically assured me of that.

The old trail twisted, widened, narrowed again, swung to the northwest and downward, into the thickening wood. The forest had changed very little. It seemed almost the same trail a young man had ridden centuries before, riding for the sheer pleasure of it, riding to explore that vast green realm which extended over most of the continent, if he did not stray into Shadow. It would be good to be doing it again for no reason other than this.

After perhaps an hour, I had worked my way well back into the forest, where the trees were great dark towers, what sunlight I glimpsed caught like phoenix nests in their highest branches, an always moist, twilight softness smoothing the outlines of stumps and boles, logs and mossy rocks. A deer bounded across my path, not trusting to the excellent concealment of a thicket at the right of the trail. Bird notes sounded about me, never too near. Occasionally, I crossed the tracks of other horsemen. Some of these were quite fresh, but they did not stay long with the trail. Kolvir was well out of sight, had been for some time.

The trail rose again, and I knew that I would shortly reach the top of a small ridge, pass among rocks, and head downward once more. The trees thinned somewhat as we climbed, until finally I was afforded a partial view of the sky. It was enlarged as I continued, and when I came to the summit I heard the distant cry of a hunting bird.

Glancing upward, I saw a great dark shape, circling and circling, high above me. I hurried past the boulders and shook the reins for a burst of speed as soon as the way was clear. We plunged downward, racing to get under cover of the larger trees once again.

The bird cried out as we did this, but we won to the shade, to the dimness, without incident. I slowed gradually after that and continued to listen, but there were

114

no untoward sounds on the air. This part of the forest was pretty much the same as that we had left beyond the ridge, save for a small stream we picked up and paralleled for a time, finally crossing it at a shallow ford. Beyond, the trail widened and a little more light leaked through and flowed with us for half a league. We had almost come a sufficient distance for me to begin those small manipulations of Shadow which would bear me to the pathway back to the shadow Earth of my former exile. Yet, it would be difficult to begin here, easier farther along. I resolved to save the strain on myself and my mount by continuing to a better beginning. Nothing of a threatening nature had really occurred. The bird could be a wild hunter, probably was.

Only one thought nagged at me as I rode.

Julian . . .

Arden was Julian's preserve, patrolled by his rangers, sheltering several encampments of his troops at all times—Amber's inland border guard, both against incursions natural and against those things which might appear at the boundaries of Shadow.

Where did Julian go when he had departed the palace so suddenly on the night of Brand's stabbing? If he wished simply to hide, there was no necessity for him to flee farther than this. Here he was strong, backed by his own men, moving in a realm he knew far better than the rest of us. It was quite possible that he was not, right now, too far away. Also, he liked to hunt. He had his hellhounds, he had his birds . . .

A half mile, a mile . . .

Just then, I heard the sound that I feared most. Piercing the green and the shade, there came the notes of a hunting horn. They came from some distance behind me, and I think from the left of the trail.

I urged my mount to a gallop and the trees rushed to a blur on either side. The trail was straight and level here. We took advantage of this.

Then from behind, I heard a roar—a kind of deep-chested coughing, growling sound backed by a lot of resonant lung space. I did not know what it was that had uttered it, but it was no dog. Not even a hellhound sounded like that. I glanced back, but there was no pursuit in sight. So I kept low and talked to Drum a bit.

After a time, I heard a crashing noise in the woods off to my right, but the roar was not repeated just then. I looked again, several times, but I was unable to make out what it was that was causing the disturbance. Shortly thereafter, I heard the horn once more, much nearer, and this time it was answered by the barks and the baying which I could not mistake. The hellhounds were coming—swift, powerful, vicious beasts Julian had found in some shadow and trained to the hunt.

It was time, I decided, to begin the shift. Amber was still strong about me, but I laid hold of Shadow as best I could and started the movement.

The trail began to curve to the left, and as we raced along it the trees at either hand diminished in size, fell back. Another curve, and the trail led us through a clearing, perhaps two hundred meters across. I glanced up then and saw that that damned bird was still circling, much nearer now, close enough to be dragged with me through Shadow.

This was more complicated than I had intended. I wanted an open space in which to wheel my mount and swing a blade freely if it came to that. The occurrence of such a place, however, revealed my position quite clearly to the bird, whom it was proving difficult to lose.

All right. We came to a low hill, mounted it, started downward, passing a lone, lightning-blasted tree as we did. On its nearest branch sat a hawk of gray and silver and black. I whistled to it as we passed, and it leaped into the air, shrieking a savage battle cry.

Hurrying on, I heard the individual voices of the dogs clearly now, and the thud of the horses' hoofs. Mixed in with these sounds there was something else, more a vibration, a shuddering of the ground. I looked back again, but none of my pursuit had yet topped the hill. I bent my mind toward the way away and clouds occluded the sun. Strange flowers appeared along the trail—green and yellow and purple—and there came a rumble of distant thunders. The clearing widened, lengthened. It became completely level.

I heard once again the sound of the horn. I turned for another look.

It bounded into view then, and I realized at that instant that I was not the object of the hunt, that the riders, the dogs, the bird, were pursuing the thing that ran behind me. Of course, this was a rather academic distinction, in that I was in front, and quite possibly the object of *its* hunt. I leaned forward, shouting to Drum and digging in with my knees, realizing even as I did that the abomination was moving faster than we could. It was a panic reaction.

I was being pursued by a manticora.

The last time I had seen its like was on the day before the battle in which Eric died. As I had led my troops up the rearward slopes of Kolvir, it had appeared to tear a man named Rall in half. We had dispatched it with automatic weapons. The thing proved twelve feet in length, and like this one it had worn a human face on the head and shoulders of a lion; it, too, had had a pair of eaglelike wings folded against its sides and the long pointed tail of a scorpion curving in the air above it. A number of them had somehow wandered in from Shadow to devil our steps as we headed for that battle. There was no reason to believe all of them had been accounted for, save that none had been reported since that time and no evidence of their continued existence in the vicinity of Amber had come to light. Apparently, this one had wandered down into Arden and been living in the forest since that time.

A final glance showed me that I might be pulled down in moments if I did not make a stand. It also showed me a dark avalanche of dogs rushing down the hill.

I did not know the intelligence or psychology of the

117

manticora. Most fleeing beasts will not stop to attack something which is not bothering them. Self-preservation is generally foremost in their minds. On the other hand, I was not certain that the manticora even realized that it was being pursued. It might have started out on my trail and only had its own picked up afterward. It might have only the one thing on its mind. It was hardly a time to pause and reflect on all the possibilities.

I drew Grayswandir and turned my mount to the left, pulling back on the reins immediately as he made the turn.

Drum screamed and rose high onto his hind legs. I felt myself sliding backward, so I jumped to the ground and leaped to the side.

But I had, for the moment, forgotten the speed of the storm-hounds, had also forgotten how easily they had once overtaken Random and myself in Flora's Mercedes, had also forgotten that unlike ordinary dogs chasing cars, they had begun tearing the vehicle apart.

Suddenly, they were all over the manticora, a dozen or more dogs, leaping and biting. The beast threw back its head and uttered another cry as they struck at it. It swept that vicious tail through them, sending one flying, stunning or killing two others. It reared then and turned, striking out with its forelegs as it descended.

But even as it did this, a hound attached itself to its left foreleg, two more were at its haunches and one had scrambled onto its back, biting at its shoulder and neck. The others were circling it now. As soon as it would go after one, the others would dart in and slash at it.

It finally caught the one on its back with its scorpion sting and disemboweled the one gnawing at its leg. However, it was running blood from a double dozen wounds by then. Shortly, it became apparent that the leg was giving it trouble, both for striking purposes and for bearing its weight when it struck with the others. In the meantime, another dog had mounted its back and

118

was tearing at its neck. It seemed to be having a more difficult time getting at this one. Another came in from its right and shredded its ear. Two more plied its haunches, and when it reared again one rushed in and tore at its belly. Their barks and growls also seemed to be confusing it somewhat, and it began striking wildly at the ever-moving gray shapes.

I had caught hold of Drum's bridle and was trying to calm him sufficiently to remount and get the hell out of there. He kept trying to rear and pull away, and it took considerable persuasion even to hold him in place.

In the meantime, the manticora let out a bitter, wailing cry. It had struck wildly at the dog on its back and driven its sting into its own shoulder. The dogs took advantage of this distraction and rushed in wherever there was an opening, snapping and tearing.

I am certain the dogs would have finished it, but at that moment the riders topped the hill and descended. There were five of them, Julian in the lead. He had on his scaled white armor and his hunting horn hung about his neck. He rode his gigantic steed Morgenstern, a beast which has always hated me. He raised the long lance that he bore and saluted with it in my direction. Then he lowered it and shouted orders to the dogs. Grudgingly, they dropped away from the prey. Even the dog on the manticora's back loosened its grip and leaped to the ground. All of them drew back as Julian couched the lance and touched his spurs to Morgenstern's sides.

The beast turned toward him, gave a final cry of defiance, and leaped ahead, fangs bared. They came together, and for a moment my view was blocked by Morgenstern's shoulder. Another moment, however, and I knew from the horse's behavior that the blow had been a true one.

A turning, and I saw the beast stretched out, great gouts of blood upon its breast, flowering about the dark stem of the lance.

Julian dismounted. He said something to the other riders which I did not overhear. They remained mounted. He regarded the still-twitching manticora, then looked at me and smiled. He crossed and placed his foot upon the beast, seized the lance with one hand, and wrenched it from the carcass. Then he drove it into the ground and tethered Morgenstern to its shaft. He reached up and patted the horse's shoulder, looked back at me, turned, and headed in my direction.

When he came up before me he said, "I wish you hadn't killed Bela."

"Bela?" I repeated.

He glanced at the sky. I followed his gaze. Neither bird was now in sight.

"He was one of my favorites."

"I am sorry," I said. "I misunderstood what was going on."

He nodded.

"All right. I've done something for you. Now you can tell me what happened after I left the palace. Did Brand make it?"

"Yes," I said, "and you're off the hook on that. He claimed Fiona stabbed him. And she was not around to question either. She departed during the night, also. It's a wonder you didn't bump into one another."

He smiled.

"I'd have guessed as much," he said.

"Why did you flee under such suspicious circumstances?" I asked. "It made it look bad for you."

He shrugged.

"It would not be the first time I've been falsely accused, suspected. And for that matter, if intent counts for anything, I am as guilty as our little sister. I'd have done it myself if I could. In fact, I'd a blade ready the night we fetched him back. Only, I was crowded aside."

"But why?" I asked.

He laughed.

"Why? I am afraid of the bastard, that's why. For a long while, I had thought he was dead, and certainly hoped so—finally claimed by the dark powers he dealt

120

with. How much do you really know about him, Corwin?"

"We had a long talk."

"And . . . ?"

"He admitted that he and Bleys and Fiona had formed a plan to claim the throne. They would see Bleys crowned, but each would share the real power. They had used the forces you referred to, to assure Dad's absence. Brand said that he had attempted to win Caine to their cause, but that Caine had instead gone to you and to Eric. The three of you then formed a similar cabal to seize power before they could, by placing Eric on the throne."

He nodded.

"The events are in order, but the reason is not. We did not want the throne, at least not that abruptly, nor at that time. We formed our group to oppose their group, because it had to be opposed to protect the throne. At first, the most we could persuade Eric to do was to assume a Protectorship. He was afraid he would quickly turn up dead if he saw himself crowned under those conditions. Then you turned up, with your very legitimate claim. We could not afford to let you press it at that time, because Brand's crowd was threatening out-and-out war. We felt they would be less inclined to make this move if the throne were already occupied. We could not have seated you, because you would have refused to be a puppet, a role you would have had to play since the game was already in progress and you were ignorant on too many fronts. So we persuaded Eric to take the risk and be crowned. That was how it happened."

"So when I did arrive he put out my eyes and threw me in the dungeon for laughs."

Julian turned away and looked back at the dead manticora.

"You are a fool," he finally said. "You were a tool from the very beginning. They used you to force our hand, and either way you lost. If that half-assed attack of Bleys's had somehow succeeded, you wouldn't have lasted long enough to draw a deep breath. If it failed, as it did, Bleys disappeared, as he did, leaving you with your life forfeit for attempted usurpation. You had served your purpose and you had to die. They left us small choice in the matter. By rights, we should have killed you—and you know it."

I bit my lip. There were many things I might say. But if he was telling something approximating the truth, he did have a point. And I did want to hear more.

"Eric," he said, "figured that your eyesight might eventually be restored—knowing the way we regenerate—given time. It was a very delicate situation. If Dad were to return, Eric could step down and justify all of his actions to anyone's satisfaction—except for killing you. That would have been too patent a move to ensure his own continued reign beyond the troubles of the moment. And I will tell you frankly that he simply wanted to imprison you and forget you."

"Then whose idea was the blinding?"

He was silent again for a long while. Then he spoke very softly, almost a whisper: "Hear me out, please. It was mine, and it may have saved your life. Any action taken against you had to be tantamount to death, or their faction would have tried for the real thing. You were no longer of any use to them, but alive and about you possessed the potentiality of becoming a danger at some future time. They could have used your Trump to contact you and kill you, or they could have used it to free you in order to sacrifice you in yet another move against Eric. Blinded, however, there was no need to slay you and you were of no use for anything else they might have in mind. It saved you by taking you out of the picture for a time, and it saved us from a more egregious act which might one day be held against us. As we saw it, there was no choice. It was the only thing we could do. There could be no show of leniency either, or we might be suspected of having some use for you ourselves. The moment you assumed any such semblance of value you would have been a dead man.

122

The most we could do was look the other way whenever Lord Rein contrived to comfort you. That was all that could be done."

"I see," I said.

"Yes," he agreed, "you saw too soon. No one had guessed you would recover your sight that quickly, nor that you would be able to escape once you did. How did you manage it?"

"Does Macy's tell Gimbel's?" I said.

"Beg pardon?"

"I said—never mind. What do you know of Brand's imprisonment, then?"

He regarded me once more.

"All I know is that there was some sort of falling out within his group. I lack the particulars. For some reason, Bleys and Fiona were afraid to kill him and afraid to let him run loose. When we freed him from their compromise—imprisonment—Fiona was apparently more afraid of having him free."

"And you said you feared him enough to have made ready to kill him. Why now, after all this time, when all of this is history and the power has shifted again? He was weak, virtually helpless. What harm could he do now?"

He sighed.

"I do not understand the power that he possesses," he said, "but it is considerable. I know that he can travel through Shadow with his mind, that he can sit in a chair, locate what he seeks in Shadow, and then bring it to him by an act of will without moving from the chair; and he can travel through Shadow physically in a somewhat similar fashion. He lays his mind upon the place he would visit, forms a kind of mental doorway, and simply steps through. For that matter, I believe he can sometimes tell what people are thinking. It is almost as if he has himself become some sort of living Trump. I know these things because I have seen him do them. Near the end, when we had him under surveillance in the palace he had eluded us once in this fashion. This was the time he traveled to the shadow

Earth and had you placed in Bedlam. After his recapture, one of us remained with him at all times. We did not yet know that he could summon things through Shadow, however. When he became aware that you had escaped your confinement, he summoned a horrid beast which attacked Caine, who was then his bodyguard. Then he went to you once again. Bleys and Fiona apparently got hold of him shortly after that, before we could, and I did not see him again until that night in the library when we brought him back. I fear him because he has deadly powers which I do not understand."

"In such a case, I wonder how they managed to confine him at all?"

"Fiona has similar strengths, and I believe Bleys did also. Between the two of them, they could apparently annul most of Brand's power while they created a place where it would be inoperative."

"Not totally," I said. "He got a message to Random. In fact, he reached me once, weakly."

"Obviously not totally, then," he said. "Sufficiently, however. Until we broke through the defenses."

"What do you know of all their byplay with me—confining me, trying to kill me, saving me."

"That I do not understand," he said, "except that it was part of the power struggle within their own group. They had had a falling out amongst themselves, and one side or the other had some use for you. So, naturally, one side was trying to kill you while the other fought to preserve you. Ultimately, of course, Bleys got the most mileage out of you, in that attack he launched."

"But he was the one who tried to kill me, back on the shadow Earth," I said. "He was the one who shot out my tires."

"Oh?"

"Well, that is what Brand told me, but it jibes with all sorts of secondary evidence."

He shrugged.

"I cannot help you on that," he said. "I simply do

124

not know what was going on among them at that time."

"Yet you countenance Fiona in Amber," I said. "In fact, you are more than a little cordial to her whenever she is about."

"Of course," he said, smiling. "I have always been very fond of Fiona. She is certainly the loveliest, most civilized of us all. Pity Dad was always so dead-set against brother-sister marriages, as well you know. It bothered me that we had to be adversaries for so long as we were. Things returned pretty much to normal after Bleys's death, your imprisonment, and Eric's coronation, though. She accepted their defeat gracefully, and that was that. She was obviously as frightened at the prospect of Brand's return as I was."

"Brand told things differently," I said, "but then, of course, he would. For one thing, he claims that Bleys is still living, that he hunted him down with his Trump and knows that he is off in Shadow, training another force for another strike at Amber."

"I suppose this is possible," Julian said. "But we are more than adequately prepared, are we not?"

"He claims further that the strike will be a feint," I continued, "and that the real attack will then come direct from the Courts of Chaos, over the black road. He says that Fiona is off preparing the way for this right now."

He scowled.

"I hope he was simply lying," he said. "I would hate to see their group resurrected and at us again, this time with help from the dark direction. And I would hate to see Fiona involved."

"Brand claimed he was out of it himself, that he had seen the error of his ways—and suchlike penitent noises."

"Ha! I'd sooner trust that beast I just slew than take Brand at his word. I hope you've had the sense to keep him well guarded—though this might not be of much avail if he has his old powers back."

"But what game could he be playing now?"

"Either he has revived the old triumvirate, a thought I like not at all, or he has a new plan all his own. But mark me, he has a plan. He has never been satisfied to be a mere spectator at anything. He is always scheming. I'd take an oath he even plots in his sleep."

"Perhaps you are right," I said. "You see, there has been a new development, whether for good or ill, I cannot yet tell. I just had a fight with Gérard. He thinks I have done Brand some mischief. This is not the case, but I was in no position to prove my innocence. I was the last person I know of to see Brand, earlier today. Gérard visited his quarters a short time ago. He says the place is broken up, there are blood smears here and there, and Brand is missing. I don't know what to make of it."

"Neither do I. But I hope it means someone has done the job properly this time."

"Lord," I said, "it's tangled. I wish I had known all of these things before."

"There was never a proper time to tell you," he said, "until now. Certainly not when you were a prisoner and could still be reached, and after that you were gone for a long while. When you returned with your troops and your new weapons, I was uncertain as to your full intentions. Then things happened quickly and Brand was back again. It was too late. I had to get out to save my skin. I am strong here in Arden. Here, I can take anything he can throw at me. I have been maintaining the patrols at full battle force and awaiting word of Brand's death. I wanted to inquire of one of you whether he was still around. But I could not decide whom to ask, thinking myself still suspect should he have died. As soon as I did get word, though, should it prove he was still living, I was resolved to have a try at him myself. Now this . . . state of affairs . . . What are you going to do now, Corwin?"

"I am off to fetch the Jewel of Judgment from a place where I cached it in Shadow. There is a way it can be used to destory the black road. I intend to try it."

126

"How can this be done?"

"That is too long a story, for a horrible thought has just occurred to me."

"What is that?"

"Brand wants the Jewel. He was asking about it, and now— This power of his to find things in Shadow and fetch them back. How good is it?"

Julian looked thoughtful.

"He is hardly omniscient, if that is what you mean. You can find anything you want in Shadow the normal way we go about it—by traveling to it. According to Fiona, he just cuts out the footwork. It is therefore *an* object, not a particular object that he summons. Besides, that Jewel is a very strange item from everything Eric told me about it. I think Brand would have to go after it in person, once he finds out where it is."

"Then I must get on with my hellride. I have to beat him to it."

"I see you are riding Drum," Julian observed. "He is a good beast, a sturdy fellow. Been through many a hellride."

"Glad to hear that," I said. "What are *you* going to do now?"

"Get in touch with someone in Amber and get up to date on everything we haven't had a chance to talk about—Benedict, probably."

"No good," I said. "You will not be able to reach him. He is off to the Courts of Chaos. Try Gérard, and convince him I am an honorable man while you are about it."

"The redheads are the only magicians in this family, but I will try. . . . You *did* say the Courts of Chaos?"

"Yes, but again, the time is too valuable now."

"Of course. Get you gone. We will have our leisure later—I trust."

He reached out and clasped my arm. I glanced at the manticora, at the dogs seated in a circle about it.

"Thanks, Julian. I— You are a difficult man to understand."

"Not so. I think the Corwin I hated must have died

127

centuries ago. Ride now, man! If Brand shows up around here, I'll nail his hide to a tree!"

He shouted an order to his dogs as I mounted, and they fell upon the carcass of the manticora, lapping at its blood and tearing out huge chunks and strips of flesh. As I rode past that strange, massive, manlike face, I saw that its eyes were still open, though glazed. They were blue, and death had not robbed them of a certain preternatural innocence. Either that, or the look was death's final gift—a senseless way of passing out ironies, if it was.

I took Drum back to the trail and began my hell-ride.

10.

Moving along the trail at a gentle pace, clouds darkening the sky and Drum's whinny of memory or anticipation. . . . A turn to the left, and uphill. . . . The ground is brown, yellow, back to brown again. . . . The trees squat down, draw apart. . . . Grasses wave between them in the cool and rising breeze. . . . A quick fire in the sky. . . . A rumble shakes loose raindrops. . . .

Steep and rocky now. . . . The wind tugs at my cloak. . . . Up. . . . Up to where the rocks are streaked with silver and the trees have drawn their line. . . . The grasses, green fires, die down in the rain. . . . Up, to the craggy, sparkling, rain-washed heights, where the clouds rush and boil like a mud-gorged river at flood crest. . . . The rain stings like buckshot and the wind clears its throat to sing. . . . We rise and rise and the crest comes into view, like the head of a startled bull, horns guarding the trail. . . . Lightnings twist about their tips, dance between them. . . . The smell of ozone as we reach that place and rush on through, the rain suddenly blocked, the wind shunted away. . . .

Emerging on the farther side. . . . There is no rain, the air is still, the sky smoothed and darkened to a proper star-filled black. . . . Meteors cut and burn, cut and burn, cauterizing to afterimage scars, fading, fading. . . . Moons, cast like a handful of coins. . . . Three bright dimes, a dull quarter, a pair of pennies, one of them tarnished and scarred. . . . Down then, that long, winding way. . . . Hoof clops clear and metallic in the

129

night air. . . . Somewhere, a catlike cough. . . . A dark shape crossing a lesser moon, ragged and swift. . . .

Downward. . . . The land drops away at either hand. . . . Darkness below. . . . Moving along the top of an infinitely high, curved wall, the way itself bright with moonlight. . . . The trail buckles, folds, grows transparent. . . . Soon it drifts, gauzy, filamentous, stars beneath as well as above. . . . Stars below on either side. . . . There is no land. . . . There is only the night, night and the thin, translucent trail I had to try to ride, to learn how it felt, against some future use. . . .

It is absolutely silent now, and the illusion of slowness attaches to every movement. . . . Shortly, the trail falls away, and we move as if swimming underwater at some enormous depth, the stars bright fish. . . . It is freedom, it is the power of the hellride that brings an elation, like yet unlike the recklessness that sometimes comes in battle, the boldness of a risky feat well learned, the rush of rightness following the finding of the poem's proper word. . . . It is these and the prospect itself, riding, riding, riding, from nowhere to nowhere perhaps, across and among the minerals and fires of the void, free of earth and air and water. . . .

We race a great meteor, we touch upon its bulk. . . . Speeding across its pitted surface, down, around, then up again. . . . It stretches into a great plain, it lightens, it yellows. . . .

It is sand, sand now beneath our movement. . . . The stars fade out as the darkness is diluted to a morning full of sunrise. . . . Swaths of shade ahead, desert trees within them. . . . Ride for the dark. . . . Crashing through. . . . Bright birds burst forth, complain, resettle. . . .

Among the thickening trees. . . . Darker the ground, narrower the way. . . . Palm fronds shrink to hand size, barks darken. . . . A twist to the right, a widening of the way. . . . Our hoofs striking sparks from cobblestones. . . . The lane enlarges, becomes a tree-lined street. . . . Tiny row houses flash by. . . . Bright shutters, marble steps, painted screens, set back beyond flagged walks. . . . Passing, a horse-drawn cart, loaded with fresh vegetables. . . . Human pedestrians turning to stare. . . . A small buzz of voices. . . .

On. . . . Passing beneath a bridge. . . . Coursing the stream till it widens to river, taking it down to the sea. . . .

Thudding along the beach beneath a lemon sky, blue clouds scudding. . . . The salt, the wrack, the shells, the smooth anatomy of driftwood. . . . White spray off the lime-colored sea. . . .

Racing, to where the place of waters ends at a terrace. . . . Mounting, each step crumbling and roaring down behind, losing its identity, joined with the boom of the surf . . . . Up, up to the flattopped, tree-grown plain, a golden city shimmering, miragelike, at its end. . . .

The city grows, darkens beneath a shadowy umbrella, its gray towers stretch upward, glass and metal flashing light through the murk. . . . The towers begin to sway. . . .

The city falls in upon itself, soundlessly, as we pass. . . . Towers topple, dust boils, rises, is pinked by some lower glow. . . . A gentle noise, as of a snuffed candle, drifting by. . . .

A dust storm, quickly falling, giving place to fog. . . . Through it, the sounds of automobile horns. . . . A drift, a brief lift, a break in the gray-white, pearl-white, shifting. . . . Our hoofprints on a shoulder of highway. . . . To the right, endless rows of unmoving vehicles. . . . Pearl-white, gray-white, drifting again. . . .

Directionless shrieks and wailings. . . . Random flashes of light. . . .

Rising once more. . . . The fogs lower and ebb. . . . Grass, grass, grass. . . . Clear now the sky, and delicate blue. . . . A sun racing to set. . . . Birds. . . . A cow in the field, chewing, staring and chewing. . . .

Leaping a wooden fence to ride a country road. . . . A sudden chill beyond the hill. . . . The grasses are dry and snow's on the ground. . . . Tin-roofed farmhouse atop a rise, curl of smoke above it. . . .

On. . . . The hills grow up, the sun rolls down, darkness dragged behind. . . . A sprinkle of stars. . . . Here a house, set far back. . . . There another, long driveway wound among old trees. . . . Headlights. . . .

Off to the side of the road. . . . Draw rein and let it pass. . . .

I wiped my brow, dusted my shirt front and sleeves. I patted Drum's neck. The oncoming vehicle slowed as it neared me, and I could see the driver staring. I gave the reins a gentle movement and Drum began walking. The car braked to a halt and the driver called something after me, but I kept going. Moments later, I heard him drive off.

It was country road for a time after that. I traveled at an easy pace, passing familiar landmarks, recalling other times. A few miles later and I came to another road, wider and better. I turned there, staying off on the shoulder to the right. The temperature continued to drop, but the cold air had a good clean taste to it. A sliced moon shone above the hills to my left. There were a few small clouds passing overhead, touched to the moon's quarter with a soft, dusty light. There was very little wind; an occasional stirring of branches, no more. After a time, I came to a series of dips in the road, telling me I was almost there.

A curve and a couple more dips. . . . I saw the boulder beside the driveway, I read my address upon it.

I drew rein then and looked up the hill. There was a station wagon in the driveway and a light on inside the house. I guided Drum off the road and across a field into a stand of trees. I tethered him behind a pair of evergreens, rubbed his neck, and told him I would not be long.

I returned to the road. No cars in sight. I crossed over and walked up the far side of the driveway, passing behind the station wagon. The only light in the house was in the living room, off to the right. I made my way around the left side of the house to the rear.

I halted when I reached the patio, looking around. Something was wrong.

The back yard was changed. A pair of decaying lawn chairs which had been leaning against a dilapidated chicken coop I had never bothered to remove were gone. So, for that matter, was the chicken coop. They had been present the last time I had passed this way. All of the dead tree limbs which had previously been strewn about, as well as a rotting mass of them I had long ago heaped to cut for firewood, were also gone.

The compost heap was missing.

I moved to the space where it had been. All that was there was an irregular patch of bare earth of the approximate shape of the heap itself.

But I had discovered in attuning myself to the Jewel that I could make myself feel its presence. I closed my eyes for a moment and tried to do so.

Nothing.

I looked again, searching carefully, but there was no tell-tale glitter anywhere in sight. Not that I had really expected to see anything, not if I could not feel it nearby.

There had been no curtains in the lighted room. Studying the house now, I saw that none of the windows had curtains, shades, shutters, or blinds. Therefore . . .

I passed around the other end of the house. Approaching the first lighted window, I glanced in quickly. Dropcloths covered much of the floor. A man in cap and coveralls was painting the far wall.

Of course.

I had asked Bill to sell the place. I had signed the necessary papers while a patient in the local clinic, when I had been projected back to my old home—probably by some action of the Jewel—on the occasion of my stabbing. That would have been several weeks ago, local time, using the Amber to shadow Earth conversion factor of approximately two and a half to one and allowing for the eight days the Courts of

Chaos had cost me in Amber. Bill, of course, had gone ahead on my request. But the place had been in bad shape, abandoned as it had been for a number of years, vandalized. . . . It needed some new window-panes, some roofing work, new guttering, painting, sanding, buffing. And there had been a lot of trash to haul away, outside as well as inside. . . .

I turned away and walked down the front slope to the road, recalling my last passage this way, half-delirious, on my hands and knees, blood leaking from my side. It had been much colder that night and there had been snow on the ground and in the air. I passed near the spot where I'd sat, trying to flag down a car with a pillow case. The memory was slightly blurred, but I still recalled the ones that had passed me by.

I crossed the road, made my way through the field to the trees. Unhitching Drum, I mounted.

"We've some more riding ahead," I told him. "Not too far this time."

We headed back to the road and started along it, continuing on past my house. If I had not told Bill to go ahead and sell the place, the compost heap would still have been there, the Jewel would still have been there. I could be on my way back to Amber with the ruddy stone hung about my neck, ready to have a try at what had to be done. Now, now I had to go looking for it, when I'd a feeling time was beginning to press once again. At least, I had a favorable ratio here with respect to its passage in Amber. I clucked at Drum and shook the reins. No sense wasting it, even so.

A half hour, and I was into town, riding down a quiet street in a residential area, houses all about me. The lights were on at Bill's place. I turned up his driveway. I left Drum in his back yard.

Alice answered my knock, stared a moment, then said, "My God! Carl!"

Minutes later, I was seated in the living room with Bill, a drink on the table to my right. Alice was out in the kitchen, having made the mistake of asking me whether I wanted something to eat.

Bill studied me as he lit his pipe.

"Your ways of coming and going still tend to be colorful," he said.

I smiled.

"Expediency is all," I said.

"That nurse at the clinic . . . scarcely anyone believed her story."

"Scarcely anyone?"

"The minority I refer to is, of course, myself."

"What was her story?"

"She claimed that you walked to the center of the room, became two-dimensional, and just faded away, like the old soldier that you are, with a rainbowlike accompaniment."

"Glaucoma can cause the rainbow symptom. She ought to have her eyes checked."

"She did," he said. "Nothing wrong."

"Oh. Too bad. The next thing that comes to mind is neurological."

"Come on, Carl. She's all right. You know that."

I smiled and took a sip of my drink.

"And you," he said, "you look like a certain playing card I once commented on. Complete with sword. What's going on, Carl?"

"It's still complicated," I said. "Even more than the last time we talked."

"Which means you can't give me that explanation yet?"

I shook my head.

"You have won an all-expense tour of my homeland, when this is over," I said, "if I still have a homeland then. Right now, time is doing terrible things."

"What can I do to help you?"

"Information, please. My old house. Who is the guy you have fixing the place up?"

"Ed Wellen. Local contractor. You know him, I think. Didn't he put in a shower for you, or something?"

"Yes, yes he did. . . . I remember."

135

"He's expanded quite a bit. Bought some heavy equipment. Has a number of fellows working for him now. I handled his incorporation."

"Do you know who he's got working at my place—now?"

"Offhand, no. But I can find out in just a minute." He moved his hand to rest on the telephone on the side table. "Shall I give him a ring?"

"Yes," I said, "but there is a little more to it than that. There is only one thing in which I am really interested. There was a compost heap in the back yard. It was there the last time I passed this way. It is gone now. I have to find out what became of it."

He cocked his head to the right and grinned around his pipe.

"You serious?" he finally said.

"Sure as death," I said. "I hid something in that heap when I crawled by, decorating the snow with my precious bodily fluids. I've got to have it back now."

"Just what is it?"

"A ruby pendant."

"Priceless, I suppose."

"You're right."

He nodded, slowly.

"If it were anyone else, I would suspect a practical joke," he said. "A treasure in a compost heap. . . . Family heirloom?"

"Yes. Forty or fifty carats. Simple setting. Heavy chain."

He removed his pipe and whistled softly.

"Mind if I ask why you put it there?"

"I'd be dead now if I hadn't."

"Pretty good reason."

He reached for the phone again.

"We've had some action on the house already," he remarked. "Pretty good, since I haven't advertised yet. Fellow'd heard from someone who'd heard from someone else. I took him over this morning. He's thinking about it. We may move it pretty quick."

He began to dial.

"Wait," I said. "Tell me about him."

He cradled the phone, looked up.

"Thin guy," he said. "Redhead. Had a beard. Said he was an artist. Wants a place in the country."

"Son of a bitch!" I said, just as Alice came into the room with a tray.

She made a *tsking* sound and smiled as she delivered it to me.

"Just a couple hamburgers and some leftover salad," she said. "Nothing to get excited about."

"Thank you. I was getting ready to eat my horse. I'd have felt bad afterward."

"I don't imagine he'd have been too happy about it himself. Enjoy," she said, and returned to the kitchen.

"Was the compost heap still there when you took him over?" I asked.

He closed his eyes and furrowed his brow.

"No," he said after a moment. "The yard was already clear."

"That's something, anyway," I said, and I began eating.

He made the call, and he talked for several minutes. I got the drift of things from his end of the conversation, but I listened to the entire thing after he had hung up, while I finished the food and washed it down with what was left in my glass.

"He hated to see good compost go to waste," Bill said. "So he pitched the heap into his pickup just the other day and took it out to his farm. He dumped it next to a plot he intends to cultivate, and he has not had a chance to spread it yet. Says he did not notice any jewelry, but then he could easily have missed it."

I nodded.

"If I can borrow a flashlight, I had better get moving."

"Sure. I will drive you out," he said.

"I do not want to be parted from my horse at this point."

"Well, you will probably want a rake, and a shovel

137

or a pitchfork. I can drive them out and meet you there, if you know where the place is."

"I know where Ed's place is. He must have tools, though."

Bill shrugged and smiled.

"All right," I said. "Let me use your bathroom, and then we had better get moving."

"You seemed as if you knew the prospective buyer."

I put the tray aside and rose to my feet.

"You heard of him last as Brandon Corey."

"The guy who pretended to be your brother and got you committed?"

" 'Pretended' hell! He is my brother. No fault of mine, though. Excuse me."

"He was there."

"Where?"

"Ed's place, this afternoon. At least a bearded red-head was."

"Doing what?"

"Said he was an artist. Said he wanted permission to set up his easel and paint in one of the fields."

"And Ed let him?"

"Yes, of course. Thought it was a great idea. That is why he told me about it. Wanted to brag."

"Get the stuff. I will meet you there."

"Right."

The second thing I took out in the bathroom was my Trumps. I had to reach someone in Amber soonest, someone strong enough to stop him. But who? Benedict was on his way to the Courts at Chaos, Random was off looking for his son, I had just parted with Gérard on somewhat less than amicable terms. I wished that I had a Trump for Ganelon.

I decided that I would have to try Gérard.

I drew forth his card, performed the proper mental maneuvers. Moments later, I had contact.

"Corwin!"

"Just listen, Gérard! Brand is alive, if that is any

138

consolation. I'm damn sure of that. This is important. Life and death. You've got to do something—fast!"

His expressions had changed rapidly while I had spoken—anger, surprise, interest ...

"Go ahead," he said.

"Brand could be coming back very soon. In fact, he may already be in Amber. You haven't seen him yet, have you?"

"No."

"He must be stopped from walking the Pattern."

"I do not understand. But I can post a guard outside the chamber of the Pattern."

"Put the guard inside the chamber. He has strange ways of coming and going now. Terrible things may happen if he walks the Pattern."

"I will watch it personally then. What is happening?"

"No time now. Here is the next thing: Is Llewella back in Rebma?"

"Yes, she is."

"Get hold of her with her Trump. She's got to warn Moire that the Pattern in Rebma has to be guarded also."

"How serious is this, Corwin?"

"It could be the end of everything," I said. "I have to go now."

I broke the contact and headed for the kitchen and the back door, stopping only long enough to thank Alice and say good night. If Brand had got hold of the Jewel and attuned himself to it, I was not certain what he would do, but I had a pretty strong hunch.

I mounted Drum and turned him toward the road. Bill was already backing out of the driveway.

11.

I cut through fields in many places where Bill had to follow the roads, so I was not all that far behind him. When I drew up, he was talking with Ed, who was gesturing toward the southwest.

As I dismounted, Ed was studying Drum.

"Nice horse, that," he said.

"Thanks."

"You've been away."

"Yes."

We shook hands.

"Good to see you again. I was just telling Bill that I don't really know how long that artist stayed around. I just figured he would go away when it got dark, and I didn't pay too much attention. Now, if he was really looking for something of yours and knew about the compost heap, he could still be out there for all I know. I'll get my shotgun, if you like, and go with you."

"No," I said, "thanks. I think I know who it was. The gun will not be necessary. We'll just walk over and do a little poking around."

"Okay," he said. "Let me come along and give you a hand."

"You don't have to do that," I said.

"How about your horse, then? What say I give him a drink and something to eat, clean him up a bit?"

"I'm sure he'd be grateful. I know I would."

"What's his name?"

"Drum."

He approached Drum and began making friends with him.

"Okay," he said. "I'll be back in the barn for a while. If you need me for anything, just holler."

"Thanks."

I got the tools out of Bill's car and he carried the electric lantern, leading me off to the southwest where Ed had been pointing earlier.

As we crossed the field, I followed the beam of Bill's light, searching for the heap. When I saw what might be the remains of one, I drew a deep breath, involuntarily. Someone must have been at it, the way the clods were strewn about. The mass would not have been dumped from a truck to fall in such a dispersed fashion.

Still . . . the fact that someone had looked did not mean he had located what he had been seeking.

"What do you think?" Bill said.

"I don't know," I told him, lowering the tools to the ground and approaching the largest aggregate in sight. "Give me some light here."

I scanned what remained of the heap, then fetched a rake and began taking it apart. I broke each clod and spread it upon the ground, running the tines through it. After a time, Bill set the lantern at a good angle and moved to help me.

"I've got a funny feeling . . ." he said.

"So do I."

". . . that we may be too late."

We kept pulverizing and spreading, pulverizing and spreading. . . .

I felt the tingle of a familiar presence. I straightened and waited. Contact came moments later.

"Corwin!"

"Here, Gérard."

"What'd you say?" said Bill.

I raised my hand to silence him and gave my attention to Gérard. He stood in shadow at the bright beginning of the Pattern, leaning upon his great blade.

"You were right," he said. "Brand did show up here, just a moment ago. I am not sure how he got in. He stepped out of the shadows off to the left, there." He gestured. "He looked at me for a moment, then turned around and walked back. He did not answer when I hailed him. So I turned up the lantern, but he was nowhere in sight. He just disappeared. What do you want me to do now?"

"Was he wearing the Jewel of Judgment?"

"I could not tell. I only had sight of him for a moment, in this bad light."

"Are they watching the Pattern in Rebma now?"

"Yes. Llewella's alerted them."

"Good. Stay on guard, then. I will be in touch again."

"All right. Corwin—about what happened earlier . . ."

"Forget it."

"Thanks. That Ganelon is one tough fellow."

"Indeed," I said. "Stay awake."

His image faded as I released the contact, but a strange thing happened then. The sense of contact, the path, remained with me, objectless, open, like a switched-on radio not tuned to anything.

Bill was looking at me peculiarly.

"Carl, what is happening?"

"I don't know. Wait a minute."

Suddenly, there was contact again, though not with Gérard. She must have been trying to reach me while my attention was diverted.

"Corwin, it is important . . ."

"Go ahead, Fi."

"You will not find what you are looking for there. Brand has it."

"I was beginning to suspect as much."

"We have to stop him. I do not know how much you know—"

"Neither do I any more," I said, "but I have the Pattern in Amber and the one in Rebma under guard. Gérard just told me that Brand appeared at the one in Amber, but was scared off."

142

She nodded her small, fine-featured face. Her red tresses were unusually disarrayed. She looked tired.

"I am aware of this," she said. "I have him under surveillance. But you have forgotten another possibility."

"No," I said. "According to my calculations, Tir-na Nog'th should not be attainable yet—"

"That is not what I was referring to. He is headed for the primal Pattern itself."

"To attune the Jewel?"

"The first time through," she said.

"To walk it, he would have to pass through the damaged area. I gather that is more than a little difficult."

"So you do know about it," she said. "Good. That saves time. The dark area would not trouble him the way it would another of us. He has come to terms with that darkness. We must stop him, now."

"Do you know any short cuts to that place?"

"Yes. Come to me. I will take you there."

"Just a minute. I want Drum with me."

"What for?"

"No telling. That is why I want him."

"Very well. Then bring me through. We can as easily depart from there as from here."

I extended my hand. In a moment, I held hers. She stepped forward.

"Lord!" said Bill, drawing back. "You were giving me doubts about your sanity, Carl. Now it's mine I wonder about. She—she's on one of the cards, too, isn't she?"

"Yes. Bill, this is my sister Fiona. Fiona, this is Bill Roth, a very good friend."

Fi extended her hand and smiled, and I left them there while I went back to fetch Drum. A few minutes later, I led him forth.

"Bill," I said, "I am sorry to have wasted your time. My brother has the thing. We are going after him now. Thanks for helping me."

I shook his hand. He said, "Corwin." I smiled.

143

"Yes, that is my name."

"We have been talking, your sister and I. Not much I could learn in a few minutes, but I know it is dangerous. So good luck. I still want the whole story one day."

"Thanks," I said. "I will try to see that you get it."

I mounted, leaned down, and drew Fiona up before me.

"Good night, Mr. Roth," she said. Then, to me, "Start riding, slowly, across the field."

I did.

"Brand says you are the one who stabbed him," I said, as soon as we had gone far enough to feel alone.

"That's right."

"Why?"

"To avoid all this."

"I talked with him for a long while. He claimed it was originally you, Bleys, and himself, together in a scheme to seize power."

"That is correct."

"He told me he had approached Caine, trying to win him to your side, but that Caine would have none of it, that Caine had passed the word along to Eric and Julian. And this led to their forming their own group, to block your way to the throne."

"That is basically correct. Caine had ambitions of his own—long-term ones—but ambitions nevertheless. He was in no position to pursue them, however. So he decided that if his lot was to be a lesser one, he would rather serve it under Eric than under Bleys. I can see his point, too."

"He also claimed that the three of you had a deal going with the powers at the end of the black road, in the Courts of Chaos."

"Yes," she said, "we did."

"You use the past tense."

"For myself and for Bleys, yes."

"That is not the way Brand tells it."

"He wouldn't."

144

"He said you and Bleys wanted to continue exploiting that alliance, but that he had had a change of heart. Because of this, he claims you turned on him and imprisoned him in that tower."

"Why didn't we just kill him?"

"I give up. Tell me."

"He was too dangerous to be allowed his freedom, but we could not kill him either because he held something vital."

"What?"

"With Dworkin gone, Brand was the only one who knew how to undo the damage he had done to the primal Pattern."

"You had a long time to get that information out of him."

"He possesses unbelievable resources."

"Then why did you stab him?"

"I repeat, to avoid all this. If it became a question of his freedom or his death, it were better he died. We would have to take our chances on figuring the method of repairing the Pattern."

"This being the case, why did you consent to cooperate in bringing him back?"

"First, I was not co-operating, I was trying to impede the attempt. But there were too many trying too hard. You got through to him in spite of me. Second, I had to be on hand to try to kill him in the event you succeeded. Too bad things worked out the way they did."

"You say that you and Bleys had second thoughts about the alliance, but that Brand did not?"

"Yes."

"How did your second thoughts affect your desire for the throne?"

"We thought we could manage it without any additional outside help."

"I see."

"Do you believe me?"

"I'm afraid that I am beginning to."

"Turn here."

I entered a cleft in a hillside. The way was narrow and very dark, with only a small band of stars above us. Fiona had been manipulating Shadow while we had talked, leading us from Ed's field downward, into a misty, moorlike place, then up again, to a clear and rocky trail among mountains. Now, as we moved through the dark defile, I felt her working with Shadow again. The air was cool but not cold. The blackness to our left and our right was absolute, giving the illusion of enormous depths, rather than nearby rock cloaked in shadow. This impression was reinforced, I suddenly realized, by the fact that Drum's hoofbeats were not producing any echoes, aftersounds, overtones.

"What can I do to gain your trust?" she said.

"That's asking quite a bit."

She laughed.

"Let me rephrase it. What can I do to convince you I am telling the truth?"

"Just answer one question."

"What?"

"Who shot out my tires?"

She laughed again.

"You've figured it out, haven't you?"

"Maybe. You tell me."

"Brand," she said. "He had failed in his effort to destroy your memory, so he decided he had better do a more thorough job."

"The version I had of the story was that Bleys had done the shooting and left me in the lake, that Brand had arrived in time to drag me out and save my life. In fact, the police report seemed to indicate something to that effect."

"Who called the police?" she asked.

"They had it listed as an anonymous call, but—"

"Bleys called them. He couldn't reach you in time to save you, once he realized what was happening. He hoped that they could. Fortunately, they did."

"What do you mean?"

"Brand did not drag you out of the wreck. You did it yourself. He waited around to be certain you were

146

dead, and you surfaced and pulled yourself ashore. He went down and was checking you over, to decide whether you would die if he just left you there or whether he should throw you back in again. The police arrived about then and he had to clear out. We caught up with him shortly afterward and were able to subdue him and imprison him in the tower. That took a lot of doing. Later, I contacted Eric and told him what had happened. He then ordered Flora to put you in the other place and see that you were held until after his coronation."

"It fits," I said. "Thanks."

"What does it fit?"

"I was only a small-town GP in simpler times than these, and I never had much to do with psychiatric cases. But I do know that you don't give a person electroshock therapy to restore memories. EST generally does just the opposite. It destroys some of the short-term ones. My suspicions began to stir when I learned that that was what Brand had had done to me. So I came up with my own hypothesis. The auto wreck did not restore my memories, and neither did the EST. I had finally begun recovering them naturally, not as the result of any particular trauma. I must have done something or said something to indicate that this was occurring. Word of it somehow got to Brand and he decided that this would not be a good thing to have happen at that time. So he journeyed to my shadow and managed to get me committed and subjected to treatment which he hoped would wipe out those things I had recently recovered. This was just partly success-ful, in that its only lasting effect was to fuzz me up for the few days surrounding the sessions. The accident may have contributed, too. But when I escaped from Porter and lived through his attempt to kill me, the process of recovery continued after I regained con-sciousness in Greenwood and left the place. I was remembering more and more when I was staying at Flora's. The recovery was accelerated by Random's taking me to Rebma, where I walked the Pattern. If this had not occurred, however, I am convinced now that it would all have come back, anyway. It might have taken somewhat longer, but I had broken through and the remembering was an ongoing process, coming faster and faster near the end. So I concluded that Brand was trying to sabotage me, and that is what fits the things you just told me."

The band of stars had narrowed, and it finally vanished above us. We advanced through what seemed a totally black tunnel now, with perhaps the tiniest flickering of light a great distance ahead of us.

"Yes," she said in the darkness before me, "you guessed correctly. Brand was afraid of you. He claimed he had seen your return one night in Tir-na Nog'th, to the undoing of all our plans. I paid him no heed at the time, for I was not even aware you still lived. It must have been then that he set out to find you. Whether he divined your whereabouts by some arcane means or simply saw it in Eric's mind, I do not know. Probably the latter. He is occasionally capable of such a feat. However he located you, you now know the rest."

"It was Flora's presence in that place and her strange liasion with Eric that first made him suspicious. Or so he said. Not that it matters, now. What do you propose doing with him if we get our hands on him?"

She chuckled.

"You are wearing your blade," she said.

"Brand told me, not all that long ago, that Bleys is still alive. Is this true?"

"Yes."

"Then why am I here, rather than Bleys?"

"Bleys is not attuned to the Jewel. You are. You interact with it at near distances, and it will attempt to preserve your life if you are in imminent danger of losing it. The risk, therefore, is not as great," she said. Then, moments later, "Don't take it for granted, though. A swift stroke can still beat its reaction. You can die in its presence."

The light ahead grew larger, brighter, but there were no drafts, sounds, or smells from that direction. Advancing, I thought of the layers upon layers of explanations I had received since my return, each with its own complex of motivations, justifications for what had happened while I was away, for what had happened since, for what was happening now. The emotions, the plans, the feelings, the objectives I had seen swirled like floodwater through the city of facts I was slowly erecting on the grave of my other self, and though an act is an act, in the best Steinian tradition, each wave of interpretation that broke upon me shifted the position of one or more things I had thought safely anchored, and by this brought about an alteration of the whole, to the extent that all of life seemed almost a shifting interplay of Shadow about the Amber of some never to be attained truth. Still, I could not deny that I knew more now than I had several years earlier, that I was closer to the heart of matters than I had been before, that the entire action in which I had been caught up upon my return seemed now to be sweeping toward some final resolution. And what did I want? A chance to find out what was right and a chance to act on it! I laughed. Who is ever granted the first, let alone the second of these? A workable approximixation of truth, then. That would be enough. . . . And a chance to swing my blade a few times in the right direction: The highest compensation I could receive from a one o'clock world for the changes wrought since noon. I laughed again and made sure my blade was loose in the sheath.

"Brand said that Bleys had raised another army—" I began.

"Later," she said, "later. There is no more time."

And she was right. The light had grown large, become a circular opening. It had approached at a rate out of proportion to our advance, as though the tunnel itself were contracting. It seemed to be daylight that was rushing in through what I chose to regard as the cave mouth.

"All right," I said, and moments later we reached the opening and passed through it.

I blinked my eyes as we emerged. To my left was the sea, which seemed to merge with the same-colored sky. The golden sun which floated/hung above/within it, bounced beams of brilliance from all directions. Behind me, now, there was nothing but rock. Our passage to this place had vanished without a sign. Not too far below and before me—perhaps a hundred feet distant—lay the primal Pattern. A figure was negotiating the second of its outer arcs, his attention so confined by this activity that he had apparently not yet noted our presence. A flash of red as he took a turn: the Jewel, hanging now from his neck as it had hung from mine, from Eric's, from Dad's. The figure, of course, was Brand's.

I dismounted. I looked up at Fiona, small and distraught, and I placed Drum's reins in her hand.

"Any advice, other than to go after him?" I whispered.

She shook her head.

Turning then, I drew Grayswandir and strode forward.

"Good luck," she said softly.

As I walked toward the Pattern, I saw the long chain leading from the cave mouth to the now still form of the griffin Wixer. Wixer's head lay on the ground several paces to the left of his body. Body and head both leaked a normal-colored blood upon the stone.

As I approached the beginning of the Pattern, I did a quick calculation. Brand had already taken several turns about the general spiral of the design. He was approximately two and a half laps into it. If we were only separated by one winding, I could reach him with my blade once I achieved a position paralleling his own. The going, however, got rougher the further one penetrated the design. Consequently, Brand was moving at a steadily decreasing pace. So it would be close. I did not have to catch him. I just had to pick up a lap and a half and obtain a position across from him.

I placed my foot upon the Pattern and moved forward, as fast as I was able. The blue sparks began about my feet as I rushed through the first curve against the rising resistance. The sparks grew quickly. My hair was beginning to rise when I hit the First Veil, and the crackling of the sparks was quite audible now. I pushed on against the pressure of the Veil, wondering whether Brand had noticed me yet, unable to afford the distraction of a glance in his direction just then. I met the resistance with increased force, and several steps later I was through the Veil and moving more easily again.

I looked up. Brand was just emerging from the terrible Second Veil, blue sparks as high as his waist. He was grinning a grin of resolve and triumph as he pulled free and took a clear step forward. Then he saw me.

The grin went away and he hesitated, a point in my favor. You never stop on the Pattern if you can help it. If you do, it costs a lot of extra energy to get moving again.

"You are too late!" he called out.

I did not answer him. I just kept going. Blue fires fell from the Pattern tracery along Grayswandir's length.

"You will not make it through the black," he said.

I kept going. The dark area was just ahead of me now. I was glad that it had not occurred over one of the more difficult portions of the Pattern this time around. Brand moved forward and slowly began his movement toward the Grand Curve. If I could catch him there, it would be no contest. He would not have the strength or the speed to defend himself.

As I approached the damaged portion of the Pattern, I recalled the means by which Ganelon and I had cut the black road on our flight from Avalon. I had succeeded in breaking the power of the road by holding the image of the Pattern in my mind as we had gone across. Now, of course, I had the Pattern itself all around me, and the distance was not nearly so great. While my first thought had been that Brand was simply trying to rattle me with his threat, it occurred to me that the force of the dark place might well be much stronger here at its source. As I came up to it, Grayswandir blazed with a sudden intensity which outshone its previous light. On an impulse, I touched its point to the edge of the blackness, at the place where the Pattern ended.

Grayswandir clove to the blackness and could not be raised above it. I continued forward, and my blade sliced the area before me, sliding ahead in what seemed an approximation of the original tracery. I followed. The sun seemed to darken as I trod the dark ground. I was suddenly conscious of my heartbeat, and perspiration formed on my brow. A grayish cast fell over everything. The world seemed to dim, the Pattern to fade. It seemed it would be easy to step amiss in this place, and I was not certain whether the result would be the same as a misstep within the intact portions of the Pattern. I did not want to find out.

I kept my eyes low, following the line Grayswandir was inscribing before me, the blade's blue fire now the only thing of color left to the world. Right foot, left foot . . .

Then suddenly I was out of it and Grayswandir swung free in my hand once again, the fires partly diminished, whether by contrast with the reilluminated prospect or for some other reasons I did not know.

Looking about, I saw that Brand was approaching the Grand Curve. As for me, I was working my way toward the Second Veil. We would both be involved in the strenuous efforts these entailed in a few more minutes. The Grand Curve is more difficult, more prolonged than the Second Veil, however. I should be free and moving more quickly again before he worked his way through his barrier. Then I would have to cross the damaged area another time. He might be free by then, but he would be moving more slowly than I would, for he would be into the area where the going becomes even more difficult.

A steady static arose with each step that I took, and a tingling sensation permeated my entire body. The sparks rose to midthigh as I moved. It was like striding through a field of electric wheat. My hair was at least partly risen by then. I could feel its stirring. I glanced back once to see Fiona, still mounted, unmoving, watching.

I pressed ahead to the Second Veil.

Angles . . . short, sharp turns. . . . The force rose and rose against me, so that all of my attention, all of my strength, was now occupied in striving against it. There came again that familiar sense of timelessness, as though this was all I had ever done, all that I ever would do. And will . . . a focusing of desire to such an intensity that everything else was excluded . . . Brand, Fiona, Amber, my own identity. . . . The sparks rose to even greater heights as I struggled, turned, labored, each step requiring more effort than the previous one.

I pushed through. Right into the black area again.

Reflexively, I moved Grayswandir down and ahead once more. Again, the grayness, the monochrome fog, cut by the blue of my blade opening the way before me like a surgical incision.

When I emerged into normal light, I sought Brand. He was still in the western quadrant, struggling with the Grand Curve, about two thirds of the way through it. If I pushed hard, I might be able to catch him just as he was coming out of it. I threw all of my strength into moving as quickly as possible.

As I made it to the north end of the Pattern and into the curve leading back, it struck me suddenly what I was about to do.

I was rushing to spill more blood upon the Pattern.

If it came to a simple choice between further damage to the Pattern and Brand's destroying it utterly, then I knew what I had to do. Yet, I felt there had to be another way. Yes . . .

I slowed my pace just a trifle. It was going to be a matter of timing. His passage was a lot rougher than mine just then, so I had an edge in that respect. My entire new strategy involved arranging our encounter at just the right point. Ironically, at that moment, I recalled Brand's concern for his rug. The problem of keeping this place clean was a lot trickier, though.

He was nearing the end of the Grand Curve, and I paced him while calculating the distance to the blackness. I had decided to let him do his bleeding over the area which had already been damaged. The only disadvantage I seemed to possess was that I would be situated to Brand's right. To minimize the benefit this would give him when we crossed blades, I would have to remain somewhat to the rear.

Brand struggled and advanced, all of his movements in slow motion. I struggled too, but not as hard. I kept the pace. I wondered as I went, about the Jewel, about the affinity we had shared since the attunement. I could feel its presence, there to my left and ahead, even though I could not see it now upon Brand's breast. Would it really act to save me across that distance should Brand gain the upper hand in our coming conflict? Feeling its presence, I could almost believe that it would. It had torn me from one assailant and found, somehow, within my mind, a traditional place of safety—my own bed—and had transported me there. Feeling it now, almost seeing the way before Brand through it, I felt some assurance that it would attempt to function on my behalf once again. Recalling Fiona's words, however, I was determined not to rely on it. Still, I considered its other functions, speculated upon my ability to operate it without contact . . .

Brand had almost completed the Grand Curve. I reached out from some level of my being and made contact with the Jewel. Laying my will upon it, I called for a storm of the red tornado variety which had destroyed Iago. I did not know whether I could control that particular phenomenon in this particular place, but

I called for it nevertheless and directed it toward Brand. Nothing happened immediately, though I felt the Jewel functioning to achieve something. Brand came to the end, offered a final exertion, and passed from the Grand Curve.

I was right there behind him.

He knew it, too—somehow. His blade was out the instant the pressure was off, he gained a couple feet faster than I thought he could, got his left foot ahead of him, turned his body, and met my gaze over the lines of our blades.

"Damned if you didn't make it," he said, touching the tip of my blade with his own. "You would never have gotten here this soon if it weren't for the bitch on the horse, though."

"Nice way to talk about our sister," I said, feinting and watching him move to parry.

We were hampered, in that neither of us could lunge without departing the Pattern. I was further hampered in not wanting to make him bleed, yet. I faked a stop thrust and he drew back, sliding his left foot along the design to his rear. He withdrew his right then, stamped it, and tried a head cut without preliminaries. Damn it! I parried and then riposted by pure reflex. I did not want to catch him with the chest cut I had thrown back at him, but the tip of Grayswandir traced an arc beneath his sternum. I heard a humming in the air above us. I could not afford to take my eyes off Brand, though. He glanced downward and backed some more. Good. A red line now decorated his shirt front where my cut had taken him. So far, the material seemed to be absorbing it. I stamped, feinted, thrust, parried, stop thrust, bound, and unbound—everything I could think of to keep him retreating. I had the psychological edge on him in that I had the greater reach and we both knew I could do more things with it, more quickly. Brand was nearing the dark area. Just a few more paces. . . . I heard a sound like a single bell chime, followed by a great roaring. A shadow suddenly fell

155

upon us, as though a cloud had just occluded the sun.

Brand glanced up. I think I could have gotten him just then, but he was still a couple of feet too far from the target area.

He recovered immediately and glared at me.

"Damn you, Corwin! That's yours, isn't it?" he cried, and then he attacked, discarding what caution he still possessed.

Unfortunately, I was in a bad position, as I had been edging up on him, preparing to press him the rest of the way back. I was exposed and slightly off-balance. Even as I parried, I realized it would not be sufficient, and I twisted and fell back.

I struggled to keep my feet in place as I went down. I caught myself with my right elbow and my left hand. I cursed, as the pain was too much and my elbow slid to the side, dropping me to my right shoulder.

But Brand's thrust had gone by me, and within blue halos my feet still touched the line. I was out of Brand's reach for a death thrust, though he could still hamstring me.

I raised my right arm, still clutching Grayswandir, before me. I began to sit up. As I did, I saw that the red formation, yellow about the edges, was now spinning directly above Brand, crackling with sparks and small lightnings, its roar now changed to a wailing.

Brand took hold of his blade by the forte and raised it above his shoulder like a spear, pointed in my direction. I knew that I could not parry it, that I could not dodge it.

With my mind, I reached out to the Jewel and up to the formation in the sky . . .

There came a bright flash as a small finger of lightning reached down and touched his blade . . .

The weapon fell from his hand and his hand flew to his mouth. With his left hand, he clutched at the Jewel of Judgment, as if he realized what I was doing and sought to nullify it by covering the stone. Sucking his fingers, he looked upward, all of the anger draining from his face to be replaced by a look of fear verging on terror. The cone was beginning to descend.

Turning then, he stepped onto the blackened area, faced south, raised both his arms and cried out something I could not hear above the wailing.

The cone fell toward him, but he seemed to grow two-dimensional as it approached. His outline wavered. He began to shrink—but it did not seem a function of actual size, so much as an effect of distancing. He dwindled, dwindled, was gone, a bare instant before the cone licked across the area he had occupied.

With him went the Jewel, so that I was left with no way of controlling the thing above me. I did not know whether it was better to maintain a low profile or to resume a normal stance on the Pattern. I decided on the latter, because the whirlwind seemed to go for things which broke the normal sequence. I got back into a sitting position and edged over to the line. Then I leaned forward into a crouch, by which time the cone began to rise. The wailing retreated down the scale as it withdrew. The blue fires about my boots had subsided completely. I turned and looked at Fiona. She motioned me to get up and go on.

So I rose slowly, seeing that the vortex above me continued to dissipate as I moved. Advancing upon the area where Brand had so recently stood, I once again used Grayswandir to guide me through. The twisted remains of Brand's blade lay near the far edge of the dim place.

I wished there were some easy way out of the Pattern. It seemed pointless to complete it now. But there is no turning back once you have set foot upon it, and I was extremely leery of trying the dark route out. So I headed on toward the Grand Curve. To what place, I wondered, had Brand taken himself? If I knew, I could command the Pattern to send me after him, once I reached the center. Perhaps Fiona had an idea. Still, he would probably head for a place where he had allies. It would be senseless to pursue him alone.

157

At least I had stopped the attunement, I consoled myself.

Then I entered the Grand Curve. The sparks shot up about me.

12.

Late afternoon on a mountain: the westering sun shone full on the rocks to my left, tailored long shadows for those to the right; it filtered through the foilage about my tomb; it countered to some extent the chill winds of Kolvir. I released Random's hand and turned to regard the man who sat on the bench before the mausoleum.

It was the face of the youth on the pierced Trump, lines now drawn above the mouth, brow heavier, a general weariness in eye movement and set of jaw which had not been apparent on the card.

So I knew it before Random said, "This is my son Martin."

Martin rose as I approached him, clasped my hand, said, "Uncle Corwin." His expression changed but slightly as he said it. He scrutinized me.

He was several inches taller than Random, but of the same light build. His chin and cheekbones had the same general cut to them, his hair was of a similar texture.

I smiled.

"You have been away a long while," I said. "So was I."

He nodded.

"But I have never really been in Amber proper," he said. "I grew up in Rebma—and other places."

"Then let me welcome you, nephew. You come at

an interesting time. Random must have told you about it."

"Yes," he said. "That is why I asked to meet you here, rather than there."

I glanced at Random.

"The last uncle he met was Brand," Random said, "and under very nasty circumstances. Do you blame him?"

"Hardly. I ran into him myself a bit earlier. Can't say it was the most rewarding encounter."

"Ran into him?" said Random. "You've lost me."

"He has left Amber and he has the Jewel of Judgment with him. If I had known earlier what I know now, he would still be in the tower. He is our man, and he is very dangerous."

Random nodded.

"I know," he said. "Martin confirmed all our suspicions on the stabbing—and it was Brand. But what is this about the Jewel?"

"He beat me to the place where I had left it on the shadow Earth. He has to walk the Pattern with it and project himself through it, though, to attune it to his use. I just stopped him from doing that on the primal Pattern in the real Amber. He escaped, however. I was just over the hill with Gérard, sending a squad of guards through to Fiona in that place, to prevent his returning and trying again. Our own Pattern and that in Rebma are also under guard because of him."

"Why does he want so badly to attune it? So he can raise a few storms? Hell, he could take a walk in Shadow and make all the weather he wants."

"A person attuned to the Jewel could use it to erase the Pattern."

"Oh? What happens then?"

"The world as we know it comes to an end."

"Oh," Random said again. Then, "How the hell do you know?"

"It is a long story and I haven't the time, but I had it from Dworkin and I believe that much of what he said."

"He's still around?"

"Later," I said.

"Okay. But Brand would have to be mad to do something like that."

I nodded.

"I believe he thinks he could then cast a new Pattern, redesign the universe with himself as chief executive."

"Could this be done?"

"Theoretically, perhaps. But even Dworkin has certain doubts that the feat could be repeated effectively now. The combination of factors was unique. . . . Yes, I believe Brand is somewhat mad. Looking back over the years, recalling his personality changes, his cycles of moods, it seems there was something of a schizoid pattern there. I do not know whether the deal he made with the enemy pushed him over the edge or not. It does not really matter. I wish he were back in his tower. I wish Gérard were a worse physician."

"Do you know who stabbed him?"

"Fiona. You can get the story from her, though."

He leaned against my epitaph and shook his head.

"Brand," he said. "Damn him. Any one of us might have killed him on a number of occasions—in the old days. Just when he would get you mad enough, though, he would change. After a while, you would get to thinking he wasn't such a bad guy after all. Too bad he didn't push one of us just a little harder at the wrong time . . ."

"Then I take it he is now fair game?" said Martin.

I looked at him. The muscles in his jaws had tightened and his eyes narrowed. For a moment, all of our faces fled across his, like a riffling of the family cards. All of our egoism, hatred, envy, pride, and abuse seemed to flow by in that instant—and he had not even set foot in Amber yet. Something snapped inside me and I reached out and seized him by the shoulders.

"You have good reason to hate him," I said, "and the answer to your question is 'yes.' The hunting season is open. I see no way to deal with him other than to destroy him. I hated him myself for so long as he remained an abstraction. But—now—it is different. Yes, he must be killed. But do not let that hatred be your baptism into our company. There has been too much of it among us. I look at your face—I don't know. . . . I am sorry, Martin. Too much is going on right now. You are young. I have seen more things. Some of them bother me—differently. That's all."

I released my grip and stepped back.

"Tell me about yourself," I said.

"I was afraid of Amber for a long while," he began, "and I guess that I still am. Ever since he attacked me, I have been wondering whether Brand might catch up with me again. I have been looking over my shoulder for years. I have been afraid of all of you, I suppose. I knew most of you as pictures on cards—with bad reputations attached. I told Random—Dad—that I did not want to meet you all at once, and he suggested that I see you first. Neither of us realized at the time that you would be particularly interested in certain things that I know. After I mentioned them though, Dad said I had to see you as soon as possible. He has been telling me all about what has been going on and—you see, I know something about it."

"I had a feeling that you might—when a certain name cropped up not too long ago."

"The Tecys?" Random said.

"The same."

"It is difficult, deciding where to start . . ." Martin said.

"I know that you grew up in Rebma, walked the Pattern, and then used your power over Shadow to visit Benedict in Avalon," I said. "Benedict told you more about Amber and Shadow, taught you the use of the Trumps, coached you in weaponry. Later, you departed to walk in Shadow by yourself. And I know what Brand did to you. That is the sum of my knowledge."

He nodded, stared off into the west.

"After I left Benedict's, I traveled for years in Shad-

162

ow," he said. "Those were the happiest times I have known. Adventure, excitement, new things to see, to do. . . . In the back of my mind, I always had it that one day when I was smarter and tougher—more experienced—I would journey to Amber and meet my other relatives. Then Brand caught up with me. I was camped on a little hillside, just resting from a long ride and taking my lunch, on my way to visit my friends the Tecys. Brand contacted me then. I had reached Benedict with his Trump, when he was teaching me how to use them, and other times when I had traveled. He had even transported me through occasionally, so I knew what it felt like, knew what it was all about. This felt the same way, and for a moment, I thought that somehow it was Benedict calling me. But no. It was Brand—I recognized him from his picture in the deck. He was standing in the midst of what seemed to be the Pattern. I was curious. I did not know how he had reached me. So far as I knew, there was no Trump for me. He talked for a minute—I forget what he said— and when everything was firm and clear, he—he stabbed me. I pushed him and pulled away then. He held the contact somehow. It was hard for me to break it—and when I did, he tried to reach me again. But I was able to block him. Benedict had taught me that. He tried again, several times, but I kept blocking. Finally, he stopped. I was near to the Tecys. I managed to get onto my horse and make it to their place. I thought I was going to die, because I had never been hurt that badly before. But after a time, I began to recover. Then I grew afraid once again, afraid that Brand would find me and finish what he had begun."

"Why didn't you contact Benedict," I asked him, "and tell him what had happened, tell him of your fears?"

"I thought of that," he said, "and I also thought of the possibility that Brand believed he had succeeded, that I was indeed dead. I did not know what sort of power struggle was going on in Amber, but I decided that the attempt on my life was probably part of such a thing. Benedict had told me enough about the family that this was one of the first things to come to mind. So I decided that perhaps it would be better to remain dead. I left the Tecys before I was completely recovered and rode off to lose myself in Shadow.

"I happened upon a strange thing then," he continued, "a thing I had never before encountered, but which now seemed virtually omnipresent: In nearly all of the shadows through which I passed, there was a peculiar black road existing in some form or other. I did not understand it, but since it was the only thing I had come across which seemed to traverse Shadow itself, my curiosity was aroused. I resolved to follow it and learn more about it. It was dangerous. I learned very quickly not to tread the thing. Strange shapes seemed to travel it at night. Natural creatures which ventured upon it sickened and died. So I was careful. I went no nearer than was necessary to keep it in sight. I followed it through many places. I quickly learned that everywhere it ran there was death, desolation, or trouble nearby. I did not know what to make of it.

"I was still weak from my wound," he went on, "and I made the mistake of pressing myself, of riding too far, too fast, in a day's time. That evening, I fell ill and I lay shivering in my blanket through the night and much of the next day. I was into and out of delirium during this time, so I do not know exactly when she appeared. She seemed like part of my dream much of the while. A young girl. Pretty. She took care of me while I recovered. Her name was Dara. We talked interminably. It was very pleasant. Having someone to talk with like that . . . I must have told her my whole life story. Then she told me something of herself. She was not a native of the area in which I had collapsed. She said that she had traveled there through Shadow. She could not yet walk through it as we do, though she felt she could learn to do this, as she claimed descent from the House of Amber through Benedict. In fact, she wanted very badly to learn how it was done. Her means of travel then was the black road itself. She was immune to its noxious effects, she said, because she was also related to the dwellers at its farther end, in the Courts of Chaos. She wanted to learn our ways though, so I did my best to instruct her in those things that I did know. I told her of the Pattern, even sketched it for her. I showed her my Trumps—Benedict had given me a deck—to show her the appearance of her other relatives. She was particularly interested in yours."

"I begin to understand," I said. "Go on."

"She told me that Amber, in the fullness of its corruption and presumption, had upset a kind of metaphysical balance between itself and the Courts of Chaos. Her people now had the job of redressing the matter by laying waste to Amber. Their own place is not a shadow of Amber, but a solid entity in its own right. In the meantime, all of the intervening shadows are suffering because of the black road. My knowledge of Amber being what it was, I could only listen. At first, I accepted everything that she said. Brand, to me, certainly fit her description of evil in Amber. But when I mentioned him, she said no. He was some sort of hero back where she hied from. She was uncertain as to the particulars, but it did not trouble her all that much. It was then that I realized how oversure she seemed about everything—there was a ring of the fanatic when she talked. Almost unwillingly, I found myself trying to defend Amber. I thought of Llewella and of Benedict—and of Gérard, whom I had met a few times. She was eager to learn of Benedict, I discovered. That proved the soft spot in her armor. Here I could speak with some knowledge, and here she was willing to believe the good things I had to say. So, I do not know what the ultimate effect of all this talk was, except that she seemed somewhat less sure of herself near the end . . ."

"The end?" I said. "What do you mean? How long was she with you?"

"Almost a week," he replied. "She had said she would take care of me until I was recovered, and she did. Actually, she remained several days longer. She said that was just to be sure, but I think it was really that she wanted to continue our conversations. Finally though, she said that she had to be moving on. I asked her to stay with me, but she said no. I offered to go with her, but she said no to that, too. She must have realized that I planned to follow her then, because she slipped away during the night. I could not ride the black road, and I had no idea what shadow she would travel to next on her way to Amber. When I awoke in the morning and realized she had gone, I thought for a time of visiting Amber myself. But I was still afraid. Perhaps some of the things she had said had reinforced my own fears. Whatever, I decided to remain in Shadow. And so I traveled on, seeing things, trying to learn things—until Random found me and told me he wanted me to come home. He brought me here first though, to meet you, because he wanted you to hear my story before any of the others. He said that you knew Dara, that you wanted to learn more about her. I hope that I have helped."

"Yes," I said. "Thank you."

"I understand that she did finally walk the Pattern."

"Yes, she succeeded in that."

"And afterward declared herself an enemy of Amber."

"That, too."

"I hope," he said, "that she comes to no harm from all this. She was kind to me."

"She seems quite able to take care of herself," I said. "But . . . yes, she is a likable girl. I cannot promise you anything concerning her safety, because I still know so little about her, so little of her part in everything that is going on. Yet, what you have told me has been helpful. It makes her someone I would still like to grant doubt's benefit, as far as I can."

He smiled.

"I am glad to hear that."

I shrugged.

"What are you going to do now?" I asked.

166

"I am taking him to see Vialle," Random said, "and then to meet the others, as time and opportunity permit. Unless, of course, something new has developed and you need me now."

"There have been new developments," I said, "but I do not really need you now. I had better bring you up to date, though. I still have a little time."

As I filled Random in on events since his departure, I thought about Martin. He was still an unknown quantity so far as I was concerned. His story might be perfectly true. In fact, I felt that it was. On the other hand, I had a feeling that it was not complete, that he was intentionally leaving something out. Maybe something harmless. Then again, maybe not. He had no real reason to love us. Quite the contrary. And Random could be bringing home a Trojan Horse. Probably though, it was nothing like that. It is just that I never trust anyone if there is an alternative available.

Still, nothing that I was telling Random could really be used against us, and I strongly doubted that Martin could do us much damage if that was his intention. No, more likely he was being as cagey as the rest of us, and for pretty much the same reasons: fear and self-preservation. On a sudden inspiration, I asked him, "Did you ever run into Dara again after that?"

He flushed.

"No," he said, too quickly. "Just that time. That's all."

"I see," I said, and Random was too good a poker player not to have noticed; so I had just bought us a piece of instant insurance at the small price of putting a father on guard against his long-lost son.

I quickly shifted our talk back to Brand. It was while we were comparing notes on psychopathology that I felt the tiny tingle and the sense of presence which heralds a Trump contact. I raised my hand and turned aside.

In a moment the contact was clear and Ganelon and I regarded one another.

"Corwin," he said, "I decided it was time to check.

167

By now, you have the Jewel, Brand has the Jewel, or you are both still looking. Which one is it?"

"Brand has the Jewel," I said.

"More's the pity," he said. "Tell me about it."

So I did.

"Then Gérard had the story right," he said.

"He's already told you all this?"

"Not in such detail," Ganelon replied, "and I wanted to be sure I was getting it straight. I just finished speaking with him." He glanced upward. "It would seem you had best be moving then, if my memories of moonrise serve me right."

I nodded.

"Yes, I will be heading for the stairway shortly. It is not all that far from here."

"Good. Now here is what you must be ready to do—"

"I know what I have to do," I said. "I have to get up to Tir-na Nog'th before Brand does and block his way to the Pattern. Failing that, I have to chase him through it again."

"That is not the way to go about it," he said.

"You have a better idea?"

"Yes, I do. You have your Trumps with you?"

"Yes."

"Good. First, you would not be able to get up there in time to block his way to the Pattern—"

"Why not?"

"You have to make the ascension, then you have to walk to the palace and make your way down to the Pattern. That takes time, even in Tir-na Nog'th—especially in Tir-na Nog'th, where time tends to play tricks anyway. For all you know, you may have a hidden death wish slowing you down. I don't know. Whatever the case, he would have commenced walking the Pattern by the time you arrived. It may well be that he would be too far into it for you to reach him this time."

"He will probably be tired. That should slow him some."

"No. Put yourself in his place. If you were Brand, wouldn't you have headed for some shadow where the time flow was different? Instead of an afternoon, he could well have taken several days to rest up for this evening's ordeal. It is safest to assume that he will be in good shape."

"You are right," I said. "I can't count on it. Okay. An alternative I had entertained but would rather not try if it could be avoided, would be to kill him at a distance. Take along a crossbow or one of our rifles and simply shoot him in the midst of the Pattern. The thing that bothers me about it is the effect of our blood on the Pattern. It may be that it is only the primal Pattern that suffers from it, but I don't know."

"That's right. You do not know," he said. "Also, I would not want you to rely on normal weapons up there. That is a peculiar place. You said yourself it is like a strange piece of Shadow drifting in the sky. While you figured how to make a rifle fire in Amber, the same rules may not apply up there."

"It is a risk," I acknowledged.

"As for the crossbow—supposing a sudden gust of wind deflected the bolt each time you shot one?"

"I am afraid I do not follow you."

"The Jewel. He walked it part way through the primal Pattern, and he has had some time to experiment with it since then. Do you think it possible that he is partly attuned to it now?"

"I do not know. I am not at all that sure how the process works."

"I just wanted to point out that if it does work that way, he may be able to use it to defend himself. The Jewel may even have other properties you are not aware of. So what I am saying is that I would not want you to count on being able to kill him at a distance. And I would not even want you to rely on being able to pull the trick you did with the Jewel again—not if he may have gained some measure of control over it."

"You do make things look a little bleaker than I had them."

"But possibly more realistic," he said.

"Conceded. Go on. You said you had a plan."

"That is correct. My thinking is that Brand must not be allowed to reach the Pattern at all, that once he sets foot upon it the probability of disaster goes way up."

"And you do not think I can get there in time to block him?"

"Not if he can really transport himself around almost instantaneously while you have to take a long walk. My bet is that he is just waiting for moonrise, and as soon as the city takes form he will be inside, right next to the Pattern."

"I see the point, but not the answer."

"The answer is that you are not going to set foot in Tir-na Nog'th tonight."

"Hold on a minute!"

"Hold on, hell! You imported a master strategist, you'd better listen to what he has to say."

"Okay, I am listening."

"You have agreed that you probably cannot reach the place in time. But someone else can."

"Who and how?"

"All right. I have been in touch with Benedict. He has returned. At this moment, he is in Amber, down in the chamber of the Pattern. By now, he should have finished walking it and be standing there at its center, waiting. You proceed to the foot of the stairs to the sky-city. There you await the rising of the moon. As soon as Tir-na Nog'th takes form, you will contact Benedict via his Trump. You tell him that all is ready, and he will use the power of the Pattern in Amber to transport himself to the place of the Pattern in Tir-na Nog'th. No matter how fast Brand travels, he cannot gain much on that."

"I see the advantages," I said. "That is the fastest way to get a man up there and Benedict is certainly a good man. He should have no trouble dealing with Brand."

"Do you really think Brand will make no other preparations?" Ganelon said. "From everything I've heard about the man, he's smart even if he is daft. He just may anticipate something like this."

"Possibly. Any idea what he might do?"

He made a sweeping gesture with one hand, slapped his neck and smiled.

"A bug," he said. "Pardon me. Pesky little things."

"You still think—"

"I think you had better remain in contact with Benedict the entire time he is up there, that is what I think. If Brand gets the upper hand, you may need to pull Benedict back immediately to save his life."

"Of course. But then—"

"But then we would have lost a round. Admitted. But not the game. Even with the Jewel fully attuned, he would have to get to the primal Pattern to do his real damage with it—and you have that under guard."

"Yes," I said. "You seem to have everything figured. You surprised me, moving so fast."

"I've had a lot of time on my hands recently, which can be a bad thing unless you use it for thinking. So I did. What I think now is that you had best move fast. The day isn't getting any longer."

"Agreed," I said. "Thanks for the good counsel."

"Save your thanks till we see what comes of it," he said, and then he broke the contact.

"That one sounded important," Random said. "What's up?"

"Appropriate question," I answered, "but I am all out of time now. You will have to wait till morning for the story."

"Is there anything I can do to help?"

"As a matter of fact," I said, "yes, if you'll either ride double or go back to Amber on a Trump. I need Star."

"Sure," Random said. "No trouble. Is that all?"

"Yes. Haste is all."

We moved toward the horses.

I patted Star a few times and then mounted.

"We'll see you in Amber," Random said. "Good luck."

"In Amber," I said. "Thanks."

I turned and headed toward the place of the stairway, treading my tomb's lengthening shadow eastward.

On the highest ridge of Kolvir there is a formation which resembles three steps. I sat on the lowest of these and waited for more to occur above me. It takes night and moonlight to do this, so half of the requirements had been met.

There were clouds to the west and northeast. I was leery of those clouds. If they massed sufficiently to block all moonlight, Tir-na Nog'th faded back to nothingness. This was one reason why it was always advisable to have a backup man on the ground, to Trump you to safety should the city vanish about you.

The sky overhead was clear, however, and filled with familiar stars. When the moon came up and its light fell upon the stone at which I rested, the stairway in the sky would come into being, sweeping upward to a great height, taking its way to Tir-na Nog'th, the image of Amber that rode the night's middle air.

I was weary. Too much had occurred in too brief a time. Suddenly to be at rest, to remove my boots and rub my feet, to lean back and rest my head, even against stone, was a luxury, a pure animal pleasure. I drew my cloak together before me against the growing chill. A hot bath, a full meal, a bed would be very good things. But these assumed an almost mythic quality from that vantage. It was more than sufficient simply to rest as I was, to let my thoughts move more slowly, drifting, spectatorlike, back over the day's happenings.

So much . . . but now, at least, I had some answers to some of my questions. Not all of them, certainly. But enough to slake my mind's thirst for the moment . . . I now had some idea as to what had been going on during my absence, a better understanding of what was happening now, a knowledge of some of the things that had to be done, of what *I* had to do. . . . And I felt, somehow, that I knew more than I realized, consciously, that I already possessed pieces that would fit the growing picture before me, if I were only to jiggle them, flip them, rotate them properly. The pace of recent events, particularly today's, had not allowed me a moment's reflection. Now, though, some of the pieces seemed to be turning at odd angles. . . .

I was distracted by a stirring above my shoulder, a tiny effect of brightening in the higher air. Turning, then standing, I regarded the horizon. A preliminary glow had occurred out over the sea at the point where the moon would ascend. As I watched, a minute arc of light came into view. The clouds had shifted slightly also, though not enough to cause concern. I glanced up then, but the overhead phenomenon had not yet begun. I withdrew my Trumps, however, riffled them, and cut out Benedict's.

Lethargy forgotten, I stared, watching the moon expand above the water, casting a trail of light over the waves. A faint form was suddenly hovering on the threshold of visibility high overhead. As the light grew, a spark limned it here and there. The first lines, faint as spider webbing, appeared above the rock. I studied Benedict's card, I reached for contact. . . .

His cold image came alive. I saw him in the chamber of the Pattern, standing at the designs' center. A lighted lantern glowed beside his left foot. He became aware of my presence.

"Corwin," he said, "is it time?"

"Not quite," I told him. "The moon is rising. The city is just beginning to take form. So it will only be a little longer. I wanted to be certain you were ready."

"I am ready," he said.

174

"It is good that you came back when you did. Did you learn anything of interest?"

"Ganelon called me back," he said, "as soon as he learned what had happened. His plan seemed a good one, which is why I am here. As for the Courts of Chaos, yes. I believe I have learned a few things—"

"A moment," I said.

The moonbeam strands had assumed a more tangible appearance. The city overhead was now clear in outline. The stairway was visible in its entirety, though fainter in some places than in others. I stretched forth enough to slake my mind's thirst for the moment . . . .

Cool, soft, I encountered the fourth stair. It seemed to give somewhat beneath my push, however.

"Almost," I said to Benedict. "I am going to try the stairs. Be ready."

He nodded.

I mounted the stone stairs, one, two, three. I raised my foot then and lowered it upon the fourth, ghostly one. It yielded gently to my weight. I was afraid to raise my other foot, so I waited, watching the moon. I breathed the cool air as the brightness increased, as the path in the waters widened. Glancing upward, I saw Tir-na Nog'th lose something of its transparency. The stars behind it grew dimmer. As this occurred, the stair became firmer beneath my foot. All resiliency went out of it. I felt that it might bear my full weight. Casting my eyes along its length, I now saw it in its entirety, here translucent, there transparent, sparkling, but continuous all the way up to the silent city that drifted above the sea. I raised my other foot and stood on the fourth stair. If I'd the mind, a few more steps would send me along that celestial escalator into the place of dreams made real, walking neuroses and dubious prophecy, into a moonlit city of ambiguous wish fulfillment, twisted time, and pallid beauty. I stepped back down and glanced at the moon, now balanced on the world's wet rim. I regarded Benedict's Trump in its silvery glow.

"The stair is solid, the moon is up," I said.

175

"All right. I am going."

I watched him there at the center of the Pattern. He raised the lantern in his left hand and for a moment stood unmoving. An instant later he was gone, and so was Pattern. Another instant, and he stood within a similar chamber, this time outside the Pattern, next to the point where it begins. He raised the lantern high and looked all around the room. He was alone.

He turned, walked to the wall, set the lantern beside it. His shadow stretched toward the Pattern, changed shape as he turned on his heel, moved back to his first position.

This Pattern, I noted, glowed with a paler light than the one in Amber—silvery white, without the hint of blue with which I was familiar. Its configuration was the same, but the ghost city played strange tricks with perspective. There were distortions—narrowings, widenings—which seemed to shift for no particular reason across its surface, as though I viewed the entire tableau through an irregular lens rather than Benedict's Trump.

I retreated down the stairs, settled once again on the lowest step. I continued to observe.

Benedict loosened his blade in its scabbard.

"You know about the possible effect of blood on the Pattern?" I asked.

"Yes. Ganelon told me."

"Did you ever suspect—any of this?"

"I never trusted Brand," he told me.

"What of your journey to the Courts of Chaos? What did you learn?"

"Later, Corwin. He could come any time now."

"I hope no distracting visions show up," I said, recalling my own journey to Tir-na Nog'th and his own part in my final adventure there.

He shrugged.

"One gives them power by paying them heed. My attention is reserved for one matter tonight."

He turned through a full circle, regarding every part of the chamber, halted when he had finished.

"I wonder if he knows you are there?" I said.

"Perhaps. It does not matter."

I nodded. If Brand did not show up, we had gained a day. The guards would ward the other Patterns, Fiona would have a chance to demonstrate her own skill in matters arcane by locating Brand for us. We would then pursue him. She and Bleys had been able to stop him once before. Could she do it alone now? Or would we have to find Bleys and try to convince him to help? Had Brand found Bleys? What the hell did Brand want this kind of power for anyhow? A desire for the throne I could understand. Yet . . . The man was mad, leave it at that. Too bad, but that's the way it was. Heredity or environment? I wondered wryly. We were all of us, to some degree, mad after his fashion. To be honest, it had to be a form of madness, to have so much and to strive so bitterly for just a little more, for a bit of an edge over the others. He carried this tendency to its extreme, that is all. He was a caricature of this mania in all of us. In this sense, did it really matter which of us was the traitor?

Yes, it did. He was the one who had acted. Mad or not, he had gone too far. He had done things Eric, Julian, and I would not have done. Bleys and Fiona had finally backed away from his thickening plot. Gérard and Benedict were a notch above the rest of us—moral, mature, whatever—for they had exempted themselves from the zero-sum power game. Random had changed, quite a bit, in recent years. Could it be that the children of the unicorn took ages in which to mature, that it was slowly happening to the rest of us but had somehow passed Brand by? Or could it be that by his actions Brand was causing it in the rest of us? Like most such questions, the benefit of these was in the asking, not the answering. We were enough like Brand that I knew a particular species of fear nothing else could so provoke. But yes, it did matter. Whatever the reason, he was the one who had acted.

The moon was higher now, its vision superimposed upon my inward viewing of the chamber of the Pattern. The clouds continued to shift, to boil nearer the moon. I thought of advising Benedict, but it would serve no other end than distraction. Above me, Tir-na Nog'th rode like some supernatural ark upon the seas of night.

. . . And suddenly Brand was there.

Reflexively, my hand went to Grayswandir's hilt, despite the fact that a part of me realized from the very first that he stood across the Pattern from Benedict in a dark chamber high in the sky.

My hand fell again. Benedict had become aware of the intruding presence immediately, and he turned to face him. He made no move toward his weapon, but simply stared across the Pattern at our brother.

My earliest fear had been that Brand would contrive to arrive directly behind Benedict and stab him in the back. I would not have tried that though, because even in death Benedict's reflexes might have been sufficient to dispatch his assailant. Apparently, Brand wasn't that crazy either.

Brand smiled.

"Benedict," he said. "Fancy . . . You . . . Here."

The Jewel of Judgment hung fiery upon his breast.

"Brand," Benedict said, "don't try it."

Still smiling, Brand unclasped his sword belt and let his weapon fall to the floor. When the echoes died, he said, "I am not a fool, Benedict. The man hasn't been born who can go up against you with a blade."

"I don't need the blade, Brand."

Brand began walking, slowly, about the edge of the Pattern.

"Yet you wear it as a servant of the throne, when you could have been king."

"That has never been high on my list of ambitions."

"That is right." He paused, only part way about the Pattern. "Loyal, self-effacing. You have not changed at all. Pity Dad conditioned you so well. You could have gone so much further."

"I have everything that I want," Benedict said.

". . . To have been stifled, cut off, so early."

"You cannot talk your way past me either, Brand. Do not make me hurt you."

The smile still on his face, Brand began moving again, slowly. What was it he was trying to do? I could not figure his strategy.

"You know I can do certain things the others cannot," Brand said. "If there is anything at all that you want and think that you cannot have, now is your chance to name it and learn how wrong you were. I have learned things you would scarcely believe."

Benedict smiled one of his rare smiles.

"You have chosen the wrong line," he said. "I can walk to anything that I want."

"Shadows!" Brand snorted, halting again. "Any of the others can clutch a phantom! I am talking of reality! Amber! Power! Chaos! Not daydreams made solid! Not second best!"

"If I had wanted more than I have, I knew what to do. I did not do it."

Brand laughed, began walking again. He had come a quarter of the way about the Pattern's periphery. The Jewel burned more brightly. His voice rang.

"You are a fool, to wear your chains willingly! But if things do not call out to you to possess them and if power holds no attraction, what of knowledge? I learned the last of Dworkin's lore. I have gone on since then and paid dark prices for greater insight into the workings of the universe. This you could have without that price tag."

"There would be a price," Benedict said, "one that I will not pay."

Brand shook his head and tossed his hair. The image of the Pattern wavered for a moment then, as a wisp of cloud crossed the moon. Tir-na Nog'th faded slightly, returned to normal focus.

"You mean it, you really mean it," Brand said, apparently not aware of the moment of fading. "I shan't test you further then. I had to try." He halted again, staring. "You are too good a man to waste

179

yourself on that mess in Amber, defending something that is obviously falling apart. I am going to win, Benedict. I am going to erase Amber and build it anew. I am going to rub out the old Pattern and draw my own. You can be with me. I want you on my side. I am going to raise up a perfect world, one with more direct access to and from Shadow. I am going to merge Amber with the Courts of Chaos. I am going to extend this realm directly through all of Shadow. You will command our legions, the mightiest military forces ever assembled. You—"

"If your new world would be as perfect as you say, Brand, there would be no need for legions. If, on the other hand, it is to reflect the mind of its creator, then I see it as something less than an improvement over the present state of affairs. Thank you for your offer, but I hold with the Amber which already exists."

"You are a fool, Benedict. A well-meaning one, but a fool nevertheless."

He began to move again, casually. He was within forty feet of Benedict. Thirty. . . . He kept moving. He finally paused about twenty feet away, hooked his thumbs behind his belt, and simply stared. Benedict met his gaze. I checked the clouds again. A long mass of them continued a moonward slide. I could pull Benedict out at any time, though. It was hardly worth disturbing him at the moment.

"Why don't you come and cut me down then?" Brand finally said. "Unarmed as I am, it should not be difficult. The fact that the same blood flows in both our veins makes no difference, does it? What are you waiting for?"

"I already told you that I do not wish to hurt you," Benedict said.

"Yet you stand ready to, if I attempt to pass your way."

Benedict simply nodded.

"Admit that you fear me, Benedict. All of you are afraid of me. Even when I approach you weaponless like this, something must be twisting your guts. You see my confidence and you do not understand it. You must be afraid."

Benedict did not reply.

". . . And you fear my blood on your hands," Brand went on, "you fear my death curse."

"Did you fear Martin's blood on your own?" Benedict asked.

"That bastard puppy!" Brand said. "He was not truly one of us. He was only a tool."

"Brand, I have no desire to kill a brother. Give me that trinket you wear about your neck and come back with me now to Amber. It is not too late to set matters right."

Brand threw back his head and laughed.

"Oh, nobly spoken! Nobly spoken, Benedict! Like a true lord of the realm! You would shame me with your excessive virtue! And what is the sticking point of this all?" He reached down and stroked the Jewel of Judgment. "This?" He laughed again and strode forward. "This bauble? Would its surrender buy us peace, amity, order? Would it ransom my life?"

He halted once more, ten feet from Benedict now. He raised the Jewel between his fingers and looked down at it.

"Do you realize the full powers of this thing?" he asked.

"Enough of th——" Benedict began, and his voice cracked in his throat.

Brand hurriedly took another step forward. The Jewel was bright before him. Benedict's hand had begun to move toward his blade, but it did not reach it. He stood stiffly now, as if suddenly transformed into a statue. Then I began to understand, but by then it was too late.

Nothing that Brand had been saying had really mattered. It had simply been a running line of patter, a distraction thrown up before him while he sought cautiously after the proper range. He was indeed partly attuned to the Jewel, and the limited control this gave

181

him was still sufficient to enable him to produce effects with it, effects which I was unaware it could produce, but of which he had known all along. Brand had carefully contrived his arrival a good distance from Benedict, tried the Jewel, moved a little nearer, tried again, kept up this movement, this testing, until he found the point where it could affect Benedict's nervous system.

"Benedict," I said, "you had better come to me now," and I exerted my will, but he did not budge nor did he reply. His Trump was still functioning, I felt his presence, I observed events because of it, but I could not reach him. The Jewel was obviously affecting more than his motor system.

I looked to the clouds again. They were still growing, they were reaching for the moon. It seemed they might come across it soon. If I could not pull Benedict out when it happened, he would fall to the sea as soon as the light was fully blocked, the city disrupted. Brand! If he became aware of it, he might be able to use the Jewel to dissipate the clouds. But to do that, he would probably have to release Benedict. I did not think he would do it. Still . . . The clouds seemed to be slowing now. This entire line of reasoning could become unnecessary. I thumbed out Brand's Trump though, and set it aside.

"Benedict, Benedict," said Brand, smiling, "of what use is the finest swordsman alive if he cannot move to take up his blade? I told you that you were a fool. Did you think I would walk willingly to my slaughter? You should have trusted the fear you must have felt. You should have known that I would not enter this place helpless. I meant it when I said that I was going to win. You were a good choice though, because you are the best. I really wish that you had accepted my offer. But it is not that important now. I cannot be stopped. None of the others has a chance, and with you gone things are going to be much easier."

He reached beneath his cloak and produced a dagger.

"Bring me through, Benedict!" I cried, but it was no use. There was no response, no strength to trump me up there.

I seized Brand's Trump. I recalled my Trump battle with Eric. If I could hit Brand through his Trump, I might be able to break his concentration sufficiently for Benedict to come free. I turned all of my faculties upon the card, preparing for a massive mental assault.

But nothing. The way was frozen and dark.

It had to be that his concentration on the task at hand, his mental involvement with the Jewel, was so complete that I simply could not reach him. I was blocked at every turn.

Suddenly, the stairway grew paler above me and I cast a quick glance at the moon. A limb of cumulus now covered a portion of its face. Damn!

I returned my attention to Benedict's Trump. It seemed slow, but I did recover the contact, indicating that somewhere, inside it all, Benedict was still conscious. Brand had moved a pace nearer and was still taunting him. The Jewel on its heavy chain burned with the light of its use. They stood perhaps three paces apart now. Brand toyed with the dagger.

". . . Yes, Benedict," he was saying, "you probably would have preferred to die in battle. On the other hand, you might look upon this as a kind of honor—a signal honor. In a way, your death will allow the birth of a new order . . ."

For a moment, the Pattern faded behind them. I could not tear my eyes from the scene to examine the moon, however. There, within the shadows and the flickering light, his back to the Pattern, Brand did not seem to notice. He took another step forward.

"But enough of this," he said. "There are things to be done, and the night grows no younger."

He stepped nearer and lowered the blade.

"Good night, sweet Prince," he said, and he moved to close with him.

At that instant, Benedict's strange mechanical right

183

arm, torn from this place of shadow and silver and moonlight, moved with the speed of a striking snake. Thing of glinting, metallic planes like the facets of a gem, wrist a wondrous weave of silver cable, pinned with flecks of fire, stylized, skeletal, a Swiss toy, a mechanical insect, functional, deadly, beautiful in its way, it shot forward with a speed that I could not follow, while the rest of his body remained steady, a statue.

The mechanical fingers caught the Jewel's chain about Brand's neck. Immediately, the arm moved upward, raising Brand high above the floor. Brand dropped the dagger and clutched at his throat with both hands.

Behind him, the Pattern faded once again. It returned with a much paler glow. Brand's face in the lantern light was a ghastly, twisted apparition. Benedict remained frozen, holding him on high, unmoving, a human gallows.

The Pattern grew dimmer. Above me, the steps began to recede. The moon was half-occluded.

Writhing, Brand raised his arms above his head, catching at the chain on either side of the metal hand that held it. He was strong, as all of us are. I saw his muscles bunch and harden. By then, his face was dark and his neck a mass of straining cables. He bit his lip; the blood ran into his beard as he drew upon the chain.

With a sharp snap followed by a rattling, the chain parted and Brand fell to the floor gasping. He rolled over once, clutching at his throat with both hands.

Slowly, very slowly, Benedict lowered his strange arm. He still held the chain and the Jewel. He flexed his other arm. He sighed deeply.

The Pattern grew even dimmer. Above me, Tir-na Nog'th became transparent. The moon was almost gone.

"Benedict!" I cried. "Can you hear me?"

"Yes," he said, very softly, and he began to sink through the floor.

"The city is fading! You've got to come to me right away!"

I extended my hand.

"Brand . . ." he said, turning.

But Brand was sinking also, and I saw that Benedict could not reach him. I clasped Benedict's left hand and jerked. Both of us fell to the ground beside the high outcrop.

I helped him to his feet. Then we both seated ourselves on the stone. For a long while, we did not say anything. I looked again and Tir-na Nog'th was gone.

I thought back over everything that had happened, so fast, so sudden, that day. A great weight of weariness lay upon me now, and I felt that my energies must be at their end, that shortly I must sleep. I could scarcely think straight. Life had simply been too crowded recently. I leaned my back against the stone once more, regarding cloud and star. The pieces . . . the pieces which it seemed should fit, if only the proper jiggle, twist, or flip were applied. . . . They were jiggling, twisting, and flipping now, almost of their own accord. . . .

"Is he dead, do you think?" Benedict asked, pulling me back from a half-dream of emerging forms.

"Probably," I said. "He was in bad shape when things fell apart."

"It was a long way down. He might have had time to work some escape along the lines of his arrival."

"Right now it does not really matter," I said. "You've drawn his fangs."

Benedict grunted. He was still holding the Jewel, a much dimmer red than it had been so recently.

"True," he finally said. "The Pattern is safe now. I wish . . . I wish that some time, long ago, something had not been said that was said, or something done that was not done. Something, had we known, which might have let him grow differently, something which would have seen him become another man than the bitter, bent thing I saw up there. It is best now if he is dead. But it is a waste of something that might have been."

I did not answer him. What he had said might or might not be right. It did not matter. Brand might have been borderline psychotic, whatever that means, and then again maybe not. There is always a reason. Whenever anything has been mucked up, whenever anthing outrageous happens, there is a reason for it. You still have a mucked-up, outrageous situation on your hands, however, and explaining it does not alleviate it one bit. If someone does something really rotten, there is a reason for it. Learn it, if you care, and you learn why he is a son of a bitch. The fact is the thing that remains, though. Brand had acted. It changed nothing to run a posthumous psychoanalysis. Acts and their consequences are the things by which our fellows judge us. Anything else, and all that you get is a cheap feeling of moral superiority by thinking how you would have done something nicer if it had been you. So as for the rest, leave it to heaven. I'm not qualified.

"We had best get back to Amber," Benedict said, "There are a great number of things that must be done."

"Wait," I said.

"Why?"

"I've been thinking."

When I did not elaborate, he finally said, "And . . .?"

I riffled slowly through my Trumps, replacing his, replacing Brand's.

"Haven't you wondered yet about the new arm you wear?" I asked him.

"Of course. You brought it from Tir-na Nog'th, under unusual circumstances. It fits. It works. It proved itself tonight."

"Exactly. Isn't the last a lot of weight to dump on poor coincidence? The one weapon that gave you a chance up there, against the Jewel. And it just happened to be a part of you—and you just happened to be the person who was up there, to use it? Trace things back and trace them forward again. Isn't there an

186

extraordinary—no, preposterous—chain of coincidences involved?"

"When you put it that way . . ." he said.

"I do. And you must realize as well as I do that there has to be more to it than that."

"All right. Say that. But how? How was it done?"

"I have no idea," I said, withdrawing the card I had not looked upon in a long, long while, feeling its coldness beneath my finger tips, "but the method is not important. You asked the wrong question."

"What should I have asked?"

"Not 'How?' but 'Who?' "

"You think that a human agency arranged that entire chain of events, up through the recovery of the Jewel?"

"I don't know about that. What's human? But I do think that someone we both know has returned and is behind it all."

"All right. Who?"

I showed him the Trump that I held.

"Dad? That *is* ridiculous! He must be dead. It's been so long."

"You know he could have engineered it. He's that devious. We never understood all of his powers."

Benedict rose to his feet. He stretched. He shook his head.

"I think you have been out in the cold too long, Corwin. Let's go home now."

"Without testing my guess? Come on! That is hardly sporting. Sit down and give me a minute. Let's try his Trump."

"He would have contacted someone by now."

"I don't think so. In fact— Come on. Humor me. What have we got to lose?"

"All right. Why not?"

He sat down beside me. I held the Trump where both of us could make it out. We stared at it. I relaxed my mind, I reached for contact. It came almost immediately.

He was smiling as he regarded us.

"Good evening. That was a fine piece of work," Ganelon said. "I am pleased that you brought back my trinket. I'll be needing it soon."